參加演講比賽，接受挑戰！

　　不會唸英文單字，只會背字母，單字很快就忘記；不會說英文，只會考試，很快就對英文沒有興趣。學英文最簡單的方法，就是背「一口氣英語」或「一口氣英語演講」。背一篇就是一篇，很有成就感，背的東西說出來最美。

　　傳統美國人寫的英語演講稿，硬梆梆，句子很長，和美國日常生活會話脫節，同學背起來很辛苦。「國中生英語演講①②」，取材自美國口語的精華，用「一口氣英語」的方式，三句一組，九句一段，同學背起來很輕鬆。句子短，說起來才有力量。每一篇演講稿有 54 句，正常速度三分鐘講完，如果背到一分半鐘內，就變成直覺，終生不會忘記，唯有不會忘記才能累積，否則背到後面，前面會忘掉。

　　只要背 20 篇以上，就可以自行排列組合成新的演講稿。用「一口氣英語」的方式，每一篇固定格式，有助於記憶。背演講的時候，自己背很辛苦，如果背給別人聽，就會使你專心。建議同學可以相互背，背熟之後，站在講台上，實際操練，可以請老師或同學做你的觀眾。演講的時候，手勢也很重要。

　　一般英語演講比賽，都是先比賽「指定題目」，再比賽「看圖即席演講」，我們另出版了「英語看圖即席演講」，有了這兩套書，同學就可以勇敢地參加「英語演講比賽」了。各地方政府、學校、社團舉辦的演講比賽很多，「一口氣英語基金會」長期提供各校「英語演講比賽」得獎同學獎學金，目的在鼓勵同學重視口說英語，拒絕「啞巴英語」，歡迎各學校申請。

　　本書雖經審慎編校，疏漏之處恐所難免，誠盼各界先進不吝指正。

劉　毅

★ Contents ★

1. My Winter Vacation

Hi, ladies and gentlemen.
I love winter vacation.
It's nice to have lots of free time.

There's so much we can do.
There's so much we can see.
There's so much fun we can have!

What do I do?
What activities do I enjoy?
Let me tell you!

---

winter〔'wɪntɚ〕
winter vacation
gentleman〔'dʒɛntḷmən〕
lots of
fun〔fʌn〕
activity〔æk'tɪvətɪ〕
let〔lɛt〕

vacation〔ve'keʃən〕
lady〔'ledɪ〕
nice〔naɪs〕
free〔fri〕
have fun
enjoy〔ɪn'dʒɔɪ〕

I can relax all day.
I can turn off the alarm clock.
I can sleep late.

There's no need to get up early for school.
No need to jump out of bed.
I can sleep as late as I want to.

I can sit on the sofa and watch TV.
There's no pressure.
I can relax and enjoy!

---

relax〔rɪ'læks〕   *all day*
turn off   alarm〔ə'lɑrm〕
alarm clock   *sleep late*
need〔nid〕   *get up*
early〔'ɝlɪ〕   jump〔dʒʌmp〕
jump out of bed   *as…as* ~
late〔let〕   sofa〔'sofə〕
pressure〔'prɛʃɚ〕

1

I can go traveling.

I don't have to stay home.

There are so many places I can go.

I can travel around Taiwan.

I can even travel abroad.

The sky is the limit!

I can just pack my bags.

I better remember my camera.

I'm sure I'll get some nice photos!

---

go + V-ing   travel ('trævl̩)

stay home   around (ə'raʊnd)

Taiwan ('taɪ'wɑn)   even ('ivən)

abroad (ə'brɔd)   sky (skaɪ)

limit ('lɪmɪt)   ***the sky is the limit***

just (dʒʌst)   pack (pæk)

bag (bæg)   ***I better + V.***

remember (rɪ'mɛmbɚ)   camera ('kæmərə)

sure (ʃʊr)   photo ('foto)

***I can meet my friends*.**

It's a chance to spend time together.

I can meet them outside of school.

I can meet my friends and go shopping.

I can meet my friends and see a movie.

I can meet my friends for a nice meal.

The city is a great place to be.

We're sure to have fun.

We'll never be bored.

---

meet〔mit〕

spend〔spɛnd〕

shop〔ʃɑp〕

meal〔mil〕

great〔gret〕

be sure to + V.

bored〔bord〕

chance〔tʃæns〕

outside of

movie〔'muvɪ〕

city〔'sɪtɪ〕

be〔bi〕

never〔'nɛvɚ〕

1

I can play sports.

I can go outside.

I can get some exercise.

Maybe I'll play basketball.

Maybe I'll play baseball.

I just hope it won't rain!

Sports are relaxing.

They can keep me fit.

They are also a lot of fun!

sport（sport）

exercise（'ɛksɚˌsaɪz）

basketball（'bæskɪtˌbɔl）

hope（hop）

relaxing（rɪ'læksɪŋ）

fit（fɪt）

outside（'aʊt'saɪd）

maybe（'mebɪ）

baseball（'besˌbɔl）

rain（ren）

keep（kip）

a lot of

I can spend time with my family.

My family is very important to me.

I need to be with them.

I can visit my grandparents.

I can visit my aunts and uncles.

I'll bet they will be happy to see me!

Winter vacation is special.

It's a wonderful time of the year.

I like it the best!

---

family ('fæməlɪ)

important (ɪm'pɔrtn̩t)　　visit ('vɪzɪt)

grandparents ('grænd͵pɛrənts)

aunt (ænt)　　uncle ('ʌŋkl̩)

bet (bɛt)　　special ('spɛʃəl)

wonderful ('wʌndəfəl)　　best (bɛst)

1. My Winter Vacation

🔊 演講解說

Hi, ladies and gentlemen.	嗨，各位先生，各位女士。
I love winter vacation.	我愛寒假。
It's nice to have lots of free time.	能夠有很多空閒時間真好。
There's so much we can do.	我們有很多事情可以做。
There's so much we can see.	我們有很多東西可以看。
There's so much fun we can have!	我們可以玩得很愉快！
What do I do?	我會做什麼？
What activities do I enjoy?	我喜歡從事什麼活動？
Let me tell you!	讓我來告訴你們！

**

winter〔ˋwɪntɚ〕*n.* 冬天　　vacation〔veˋkeʃən〕*n.* 假期

winter vacation 寒假　　lady〔ˋledɪ〕*n.* 女士

gentleman〔ˋdʒɛntḷmən〕*n.* 先生

nice〔naɪs〕*adj.* 好的；漂亮的；美味的　　*lots of* 很多

free〔fri〕*adj.* 空閒的　　fun〔fʌn〕*n.* 樂趣

have fun 玩得愉快　　activity〔ækˋtɪvətɪ〕*n.* 活動

enjoy〔ɪnˋdʒɔɪ〕*v.* 享受；喜歡　　let〔lɛt〕*v.* 讓

I can relax all day.	我可以整天放鬆。
I can turn off the alarm clock.	我可以關掉鬧鐘。
I can sleep late.	我可以睡到很晚。
There's no need to get up early for school.	沒必要早起去上學。
No need to jump out of bed.	不必從床上跳起來。
I can sleep as late as I want to.	我想睡多晚就睡多晚。
I can sit on the sofa and watch TV.	我可以坐在沙發上看電視。
There's no pressure.	沒有壓力。
I can relax and enjoy!	我可以放鬆和享受！

**

relax〔rɪ'læks〕*v.* 放鬆　***all day*** 整天
turn off 關掉　　alarm〔ə'lɑrm〕*n.* 鬧鐘
alarm clock 鬧鐘　　***sleep late*** 睡到很晚
need〔nid〕*v. n.* 需要；必要　　***get up*** 起床
early〔'ɝlɪ〕*adv.* 早　　jump〔dʒʌmp〕*v.* 跳
jump out of bed 從床上跳起來　　***as…as~*** 像~一樣…
late〔let〕*adj.* 晚的　　sofa〔'sofə〕*n.* 沙發
pressure〔'prɛʃɚ〕*n.* 壓力

1

I can go traveling.　　　　　　　我可以去旅行。

I don't have to stay home.　　　　我不必待在家裡。

There are so many places　　　　我有很多地方可以去。
　I can go.

I can travel around Taiwan.　　　我可以在台灣各地旅行。

I can even travel abroad.　　　　我甚至可以到國外旅行。

The sky is the limit!　　　　　　沒有任何限制！

I can just pack my bags.　　　　我只要打包我的行李。

I better remember my camera.　　我最好要記得我的相機。

I'm sure I'll get some nice　　　我確定我會拍到一些漂亮的
　photos!　　　　　　　　　　照片！

** ─────────────────────

go + V-ing 去…　　travel〔ˋtrævḷ〕*v.* 旅行

stay home 待在家裡　　around〔əˋraʊnd〕*prep.* 在…四處

Taiwan〔ˋtaɪˋwɑn〕*n.* 台灣　　even〔ˋivən〕*adv.* 甚至

abroad〔əˋbrɔd〕*adv.* 到國外　　sky〔skaɪ〕*n.* 天空

limit〔ˋlɪmɪt〕*n.* 限制

The sky is the limit! 沒有任何限制；一切都是可能的！

just〔dʒʌst〕*adv.* 只　　pack〔pæk〕*v.* 打包

bag〔bæg〕*n.* 行李

I better + V. 我最好…（ = *I had better + V*.）

remember〔rɪˋmɛmbɚ〕*v.* 記得　　camera〔ˋkæmərə〕*n.* 相機

sure〔ʃʊr〕*adj.* 確定的　　photo〔ˋfoto〕*n.* 照片（ = *photograph*）

I can meet my friends.	我可以和我的朋友見面。
It's a chance to spend time together.	這是一個可以聚在一起的機會。
I can meet them outside of school.	我可以在校外和他們見面。
I can meet my friends and go shopping.	我可以和朋友見面，然後去逛街。
I can meet my friends and see a movie.	我可以和朋友見面，然後去看電影。
I can meet my friends for a nice meal.	我可以和朋友見面，然後去吃一頓好吃的。
The city is a great place to be.	這個城市是一個可以逗留的好地方。
We're sure to have fun.	我們一定會玩得很愉快。
We'll never be bored.	我們絕不會感到無聊。

＊＊─────────────────────

meet〔mit〕*v.* 會見　　chance〔tʃæns〕*n.* 機會

spend〔spɛnd〕*v.* 花費；度過（時間）

outside of 在⋯外面　　shop〔ʃɑp〕*v.* 購物

movie〔'muvɪ〕*n.* 電影　　meal〔mil〕*n.* 一餐

city〔'sɪtɪ〕*n.* 城市　　great〔gret〕*adj.* 很棒的

be〔bi〕*v.* 逗留；待　　***be sure to*** + ***V.*** 一定⋯

never〔'nɛvɚ〕*adv.* 絕不　　bored〔bord〕*adj.* 覺得無聊的

I can play sports.	我可以運動。
I can go outside.	我可以到戶外。
I can get some exercise.	我可以做一些鍛鍊。
Maybe I'll play basketball.	也許我會打籃球。
Maybe I'll play baseball.	也許我會打棒球。
I just hope it won't rain!	我只希望不會下雨！
Sports are relaxing.	運動可以讓人放鬆。
They can keep me fit.	它們可以讓我保持健康。
They are also a lot of fun!	它們也很有趣！

1

** ——————————

sport〔sport〕*n.* 運動

outside〔'aʊt'saɪd〕*adv.* 到戶外

exercise〔'ɛksɚ͵saɪz〕*n.* 運動；鍛鍊

maybe〔'mebɪ〕*adv.* 也許

basketball〔'bæskɪt͵bɔl〕*n.* 籃球

baseball〔'bes͵bɔl〕*n.* 棒球

hope〔hop〕*v.* 希望　　rain〔ren〕*v.* 下雨

relaxing〔rɪ'læksɪŋ〕*adj.* 使人放鬆的

keep〔kip〕*v.* 使保持（某種狀態）

fit〔fɪt〕*adj.* 健康的　　***a lot of*** 許多

I can spend time with my family.	我可以花時間陪我的家人。
My family is very important to me.	我的家人對我來說很重要。
I need to be with them.	我必須和他們在一起。
I can visit my grandparents.	我可以拜訪我的祖父母。
I can visit my aunts and uncles.	我可以拜訪我的阿姨和叔叔。
I'll bet they will be happy to see me!	我確信他們看到我會很高興！
Winter vacation is special.	寒假很特別。
It's a wonderful time of the year.	它是一年當中很棒的一段時光。
I like it the best!	我最喜歡它了！

** ——————————————

family〔ˈfæməlɪ〕*n.* 家人
important〔ɪmˈpɔrtn̩t〕*adj.* 重要的　　visit〔ˈvɪzɪt〕*v.* 拜訪
grandparents〔ˈgrændˌpɛrənts〕*n. pl.* 祖父母
aunt〔ænt〕*n.* 阿姨　　uncle〔ˈʌŋkl̩〕*n.* 叔叔
bet〔bɛt〕*v.* 打賭；確信　　special〔ˈspɛʃəl〕*adj.* 特別的
wonderful〔ˈwʌndɚfəl〕*adj.* 極好的
best〔bɛst〕*adv.* 最（= *most*）

📄 **背景說明**

　　如果寒假來臨，你會怎麼利用這個長假呢？平常課業繁重，忙到沒時間休息，很多人都想趁這時候玩個痛快。玩樂之前，先規劃好你的假期，這樣才能過一個快樂而充實的寒假生活！

1. *I can sleep late.*

   sleep late 睡到很晚

   　這句話的意思是「我可以睡到很晚。」也可說成：

   > I can sleep in. (我可以只是睡到很晚。)
   >
   > I can stay in bed. (我可以只是躺在床上。)
   >
   > I can keep on sleeping.
   >
   > (我可以只是一直睡覺。)

   sleep in 睡到很晚起床；睡懶覺　　stay〔 ste 〕*v.* 停留

   keep on + *V-ing* 持續…；一直…

2. *No need to jump out of bed.*

   need〔 nid 〕*n.* 需要；必要　　jump〔 dʒʌmp 〕*v.* 跳

   jump out of bed 從床上跳起來

   　這句話的意思是「不必從床上跳起來。」相信大家都有類似的經驗，當你心裡一直想著有事情要去做或有壓力時，有時就會從睡夢中驚醒。這句話也可說成：

No need to get up.（不必起床。）

I don't have to hurry and get up.

（我不必趕著起床。）

I don't have to start my day immediately.

（我不必馬上開始我的一天。）

get up 起床　　hurry〔ˈhɝɪ〕*v.* 趕快
start〔stɑrt〕*v.* 開始
immediately〔ɪˈmidɪɪtlɪ〕*adv.* 立刻

3. *The sky is the limit!*

sky〔skaɪ〕*n.* 天空　　limit〔ˈlɪmɪt〕*n.* 限制

The sky is the limit! 沒有任何限制；一切都是可能的！

　　這句話字面的意思是「天空是限制！」不論是陸地還是海洋，就算它們再大，終究還是有盡頭，但是天空卻沒有任何邊界，所以這句話引申為「沒有任何限制；一切都是可能的！」也可說成：

There is no limit!（沒有限制！）

Anything is possible!（什麼事都是有可能的！）

There is no end to the possibilities!

（有無窮無盡的可能！）

anything〔ˈɛnɪˌθɪŋ〕*pron.* 任何東西；什麼都
possible〔ˈpɑsəbļ〕*adj.* 可能的
end〔ɛnd〕*n.* 結束；限度
possibility〔ˌpɑsəˈbɪlətɪ〕*n.* 可能性；可能的事

1

4. *I can just pack my bags.*

pack〔pæk〕*v.* 打包　　bag〔bæg〕*n.* 行李

　　bag 的基本意思是「袋子」，在此是作「行李」解，相當於 baggage〔'bægɪdʒ〕或 luggage〔'lʌgɪdʒ〕，但這三個名詞中，只有 bag 是可數名詞，字尾可加 s。這句話的意思是「我只要打包我的行李。」也可說成：

　　I can just pack my suitcase.（我只要打包我的行李箱。）
　　I can just put some things in a bag.
　　（我只要把一些東西放進行李中。）
　　I can just pack up my stuff.
　　（我只要收拾我自己的東西。）

　　suitcase〔'sut,kes〕*n.* 手提箱；行李箱
　　pack up 收拾　　stuff〔stʌf〕*n.* 東西

5. *I better remember my camera.*

I better + V. 我最好…（ = *I had better + V.* ）
remember〔rɪ'mɛmbɚ〕*v.* 記得
camera〔'kæmərə〕*n.* 相機

　　這句話的意思是「我最好要記得我的相機。」也可說成：

　　I have to pack my camera, too.
　　（我也必須打包我的相機。）
　　I have to take my camera along.
　　（我必須帶我的相機一起去。）
　　I can't forget my camera!（我不可能忘記我的相機！）

　　have to 必須　　along〔ə'lɔŋ〕*adv.* 一起
　　forget〔fɚ'gɛt〕*v.* 忘記

6. ***I'm sure I'll get some nice photos!***

sure〔ʃur〕*adj.* 確定的

nice〔naɪs〕*adj.* 好的；漂亮的

photo〔'foto〕*n.* 照片（ = *photograph* ）

這句話的意思是「我確定我會拍到一些漂亮的照片！」
也可說成：

I'm sure I'll be able to take some nice pictures!
（我確定我能拍到一些漂亮的照片！）

I'm sure to get some good shots!
（我一定會拍到一些不錯的照片！）

I'm certain that I'll take some nice photographs!
（我確定我會拍到一些漂亮的照片！）

be able to 能夠　　take〔tek〕*v.* 拍（照）

picture〔'pɪktʃ⋅〕*n.* 照片　　***be sure to* + *V.*** 一定…

shot〔ʃɑt〕*n.* 照片　　certain〔'sɝtn̩〕*adj.* 確定的

photograph〔'fotə,græf〕*n.* 照片

7. ***The city is a great place to be.***

city〔'sɪtɪ〕*n.* 城市　　great〔gret〕*adj.* 很棒的

be〔bi〕*v.* 逗留；待

be 的基本意思是「是；成為」，在此是作「逗留；
待」解。這句話的意思是「這個城市是一個可以逗留的
好地方。」也可說成：

The city is a great place to spend time in.
（這個城市是一個可以度過時間的好地方。）

The city is a fun place to go.
（這個城市是一個可以去的有趣地方。）

The city is an interesting place to visit.
（這個城市是一個可以遊覽的有趣的地方。）

spend〔spɛnd〕*v.* 花費；度過（時間）
fun〔fʌn〕*adj.* 有趣的
interesting〔'ɪntrɪstɪŋ〕*adj.* 有趣的
visit〔'vɪsɪt〕*v.* 拜訪；遊覽

8. *They can keep me fit.*

　　keep〔kip〕*v.* 使保持（某種狀態）　　fit〔fɪt〕*adj.* 健康的

　　keep 的基本意思是「保存」，在此是作「使保持（某種狀態）」解。這句話的意思是「它們可以讓我保持健康。」也可說成：

They can keep me in shape.
（它們可以讓我保持健康。）

They can help me stay healthy.
（它們可以幫助我保持健康。）

They can keep me in top form.
（它們可以讓我非常健康。）

in shape 健康的　　stay〔ste〕*v.* 保持
healthy〔'hɛlθɪ〕*adj.* 健康的
form〔fɔrm〕*n.* 健康狀況　　*in top form* 健康極佳

keep「使保持（某種狀態）」，其用法舉例如下：

The magician *kept* the children interested.
（魔術師使小孩感興趣。）

Mrs. Jones *keeps* her husband on a strict diet.
（瓊斯太太使丈夫持續嚴格節食。）

John *keeps* his girlfriend happy with small gifts.
（約翰用小禮物使女朋友保持快樂。）

magician〔məˈdʒɪʃən〕*n.* 魔術師
children〔ˈtʃɪldrən〕*n. pl.* 小孩【單數是 child】
interested〔ˈɪntrɪstɪd〕*adj.* 感興趣的
husband〔ˈhʌzbənd〕*n.* 丈夫　　strict〔strɪkt〕*adj.* 嚴格的
diet〔ˈdaɪət〕*n.* 飲食；飲食限制　　*be on a diet* 節食
girlfriend〔ˈgɜl͵frɛnd〕*n.* 女朋友　　gift〔gɪft〕*n.* 禮物

9. *I'll bet they will be happy to see me!*

bet〔bɛt〕*v.* 打賭；確信

　　　　bet 的基本意思是「打賭」，在此是作「確信」解。這句話的意思是「我確信他們看到我會很高興！」也可說成：

I'm sure they'll be happy to have me.
（我確定他們會樂於迎接我。）

I'm certain they'd like me to come.
（我確定他們會喜歡我去。）

They're sure to be pleased to see me.
（他們一定會很高興看到我。）

【have〔hæv〕*v.* 有；迎接　　pleased〔plizd〕*adj.* 高興的】

 作文範例

My Winter Vacation

Winter vacation is a wonderful time of year. We have a lot of free time and there is so much we can do. There are some special things that I like to do during this holiday.

When winter vacation comes, I like to spend it doing the things I enjoy. These include relaxing all day. There is no need to get up early for school, so I turn off my alarm. I sleep late and then just watch TV or read a comic book. But I also like to go traveling. It's a good opportunity to see Taiwan, or even a foreign country. Another thing I like to do is meet up with my friends. We get together for a movie or a meal and just enjoy our free time in the city. Sometimes we play sports. It's a good way to relax and stay fit at the same time. ***Finally***, I spend time with my family. I visit relatives and have fun just being with them.

Winter vacation is a special time of year. With so many interesting things to do, I never feel bored. I only wish that the rest of the year were half this much fun.

📖 中文翻譯

我的寒假

寒假是一年之中一段很棒的時光。我們有很多空閒時間，而且有很多事情可以做。有一些特別的事情，我喜歡在寒假期間做。

當寒假來臨時，我喜歡把它用來做我喜歡的事情。這些包括放鬆一整天。沒有早起上學的必要，所以我會把鬧鐘關掉。我會睡得很晚，然後只看電視或看漫畫書。但我也喜歡去旅行。這是一個遊覽台灣的好機會，或甚至是外國。另一件我喜歡做的事，是和朋友見面。我們會聚在一起看電影或吃頓飯，然後就在城市中享受我們的空閒時間。有時候我們會運動。這是一個能同時放鬆又保持健康的好方法。最後，我會花時間陪家人。我會拜訪親戚，而且和他們在一起就能玩得很愉快。

寒假是一年當中的一段特別時光。有這麼多有趣的事情可以做，我絕不會覺得無聊。我只希望一年裡面的其餘時間，能有它一半好玩。

2. *My Interests*

Hello, ladies and gentlemen.

We are all special.

We all have our own interests.

Maybe we like cooking.

Maybe we like playing the piano.

There are just so many things to like!

Today, I would like to give a speech.

I'd like you to know more about me.

I'd like to tell you about my interests.

---

interest (ˈɪntrɪst)   special (ˈspɛʃəl)

own (on)   cook (kʊk)

piano (pɪˈæno)   just (dʒʌst)

would like   speech (spitʃ)

give a speech

I really like music.

I love listening to songs.

I love watching music videos.

Music is wonderful.

It can free my mind.

It can open my heart.

I can dance to the beat.

I can sing along.

Music puts me in a good mood.

---

really ('riəlɪ)

listen ('lɪsn̩)

video ('vɪdɪ,o)

wonderful ('wʌndəfəl)

mind (maɪnd)

heart (hɑrt)

to (tu)

sing (sɪŋ)

put (pʊt)

in a good mood

music ('mjuzɪk)

song (sɔŋ)

music video

free (fri)

open ('opən)

dance (dæns)

beat (bit)

along (ə'lɔŋ)

mood (mud)

I really like movies.

I like all kinds of movies.

I like to watch different movies at
different times.

Sometimes I like comedies.

Sometimes I like action movies.

Sometimes I like scary movies.

Movies are magical.

The stories are great.

The actors are larger-than-life!

---

movie ('muvɪ)

all kinds of

sometimes ('sʌm͵taɪmz)

action ('ækʃən)

scary ('skɛrɪ)

magical ('mædʒɪkḷ)

great (gret)

larger-than-life ('lardʒə-ðən'laɪf)

kind (kaɪnd)

different ('dɪfrənt)

comedy ('kamədɪ)

action movie

scary movie

story ('storɪ)

actor ('æktə-)

I love to read.

I love reading somewhere quiet.

Reading takes me to another world.

There are fantasy books.

There are mystery books.

There are even comic books.

I can also learn a lot from reading.

Good books can be educational.

Who says learning can't be fun?

---

somewhere ('sʌm,hwɛr)　　quiet ('kwaɪət)

world (wɝld)　　fantasy ('fæntəsɪ)

fantasy book　　mystery ('mɪstrɪ)

even ('ivən)　　comic ('kɑmɪk)

learn (lɝn)　　*a lot*

educational (,ɛdʒə'keʃənḷ)　　fun (fʌn)

2

I like playing games.
They can be video games.
They can be board games.

I always try my best.
There's no need to cheat!
Games are only fun if they are fair.

It doesn't matter if I win or lose.
I always have a good time.
Games can bring me closer to
my friends.

game〔gem〕   *video game*
board〔bord〕   *board game*
try one's best   cheat〔tʃit〕
fair〔fɛr〕   matter〔'mætə〕
win〔wɪn〕   lose〔luz〕
have a good time   close〔klos〕
close to

I have many interests.

My interests make life fun.

I enjoy them very much.

I know I can't always play.

Working hard is important.

But sometimes I need to relax.

We can find our own interests.

We can learn more about them.

They can make life more exciting!

---

life〔 laɪf 〕

hard〔 hɑrd 〕

important〔 ɪmˋpɔrtṇt 〕

find〔 faɪnd 〕

exciting〔 ɪkˋsaɪtɪŋ 〕

enjoy〔 ɪnˋdʒɔɪ 〕

work hard

relax〔 rɪˋlæks 〕

learn〔 lɝn 〕

2. My Interests

🔊 演講解說

Hello, ladies and gentlemen.　哈囉，各位先生，各位女士。
We are all special.　我們都很特別。
We all have our own interests.　我們都有自己的興趣。

Maybe we like cooking.　或許我們喜歡做菜。
Maybe we like playing the piano.　或許我們喜歡彈鋼琴。
There are just so many things to like!　真的有很多事物可以喜歡！

Today, I would like to give a speech.　今天，我想要發表演說。
I'd like you to know more about me.　我想要讓你們更了解我。
I'd like to tell you about my interests.　我想要告訴你們我的興趣。

** ────────────────────

interest〔ˈɪntrɪst〕n. 興趣　　special〔ˈspɛʃəl〕adj. 特別的
own〔on〕adj. 自己的　　cook〔kʊk〕v. 做菜
piano〔pɪˈæno〕n. 鋼琴　　just〔dʒʌst〕adv. 真地
would like 想要（= *want*）　　speech〔spitʃ〕n. 演說
give a speech 發表演說

I really like music.	我真的很喜歡音樂。
I love listening to songs.	我愛聽歌。
I love watching music videos.	我愛看音樂錄影帶。
Music is wonderful.	音樂是很棒的。
It can free my mind.	它可以釋放我的心靈。
It can open my heart.	它可以使我的心胸變開闊。
I can dance to the beat.	我會隨著節拍跳舞。
I can sing along.	我會一起唱歌。
Music puts me in a good mood.	音樂使我心情很好。

** ——————————————

really〔ˈriəlɪ〕*adv.* 真地　　music〔ˈmjuzɪk〕*n.* 音樂

listen〔ˈlɪsn̩〕*v.* 聽　　song〔sɔŋ〕*n.* 歌曲

video〔ˈvɪdɪˏo〕*n.* 錄影帶　　*music video* 音樂錄影帶

wonderful〔ˈwʌndɚfəl〕*adj.* 極好的；很棒的

free〔fri〕*v.* 釋放　　mind〔maɪnd〕*n.* 心靈；想法

open〔ˈopən〕*v.* 打開；使開闊　　heart〔hɑrt〕*n.* 心

dance〔dæns〕*v.* 跳舞　　to〔tu〕*prep.* 隨著

beat〔bit〕*n.* 拍子　　sing〔sɪŋ〕*v.* 唱歌

along〔əˈlɔŋ〕*adv.* 一起　　put〔put〕*v.* 使處於（某種狀態）

mood〔mud〕*n.* 心情　　*in a good mood* 心情好

I really like movies.

我真的很喜歡電影。

I like all kinds of movies.

我喜歡各種電影。

I like to watch different movies
　at different times.

我喜歡在不同的時間看不同
的電影。

Sometimes I like comedies.

有時候我喜歡喜劇片。

Sometimes I like action movies.

有時候我喜歡動作片。

Sometimes I like scary movies.

有時候我喜歡恐怖片。

Movies are magical.

電影非常神奇。

The stories are great.

情節很棒。

The actors are larger-than-life!

演員都令人印象非常深刻！

** ────────────────

movie〔ˈmuvɪ〕*n.* 電影　　kind〔kaɪnd〕*n.* 種類

all kinds of 各種的　　different〔ˈdɪfrənt〕*adj.* 不同的

sometimes〔ˈsʌmˌtaɪmz〕*adv.* 有時候

comedy〔ˈkɑmədɪ〕*n.* 喜劇　　action〔ˈækʃən〕*n.* 動作

action movie 動作片　　scary〔ˈskɛrɪ〕*adj.* 可怕的；恐怖的

scary movie 恐怖片　　magical〔ˈmædʒɪkḷ〕*adj.* 神奇的

story〔ˈstorɪ〕*n.* 故事；情節　　great〔gret〕*adj.* 很棒的

actor〔ˈæktɚ〕*n.* 演員

larger-than-life〔ˈlɑrdʒəðənˈlaɪf〕*adj.* 令人印象極深刻的；
　有英雄色彩的

I love to read.	我喜愛閱讀。
I love reading somewhere quiet.	我喜歡在安靜的地方看書。
Reading takes me to another world.	閱讀帶領我到另一個世界。
There are fantasy books.	有幻想小說。
There are mystery books.	有推理小說。
There are even comic books.	甚至有漫畫書。
I can also learn a lot from reading.	我也可以從閱讀中學到很多。
Good books can be educational.	好書是有教育意義的。
Who says learning can't be fun?	誰說學習不可能是有趣的呢？

**

somewhere〔'sʌm,hwɛr〕*adv.* 在某處

quiet〔'kwaɪət〕*adj.* 安靜的　　world〔wɝld〕*n.* 世界

fantasy〔'fæntəsɪ〕*n.* 幻想；幻想作品

fantasy book 幻想小說　　mystery〔'mɪstrɪ〕*n.* 推理小說

even〔'ivən〕*adv.* 甚至　　comic〔'kɑmɪk〕*adj.* 漫畫的

learn〔lɝn〕*v.* 學習　　*a lot* 很多

educational〔,ɛdʒə'keʃənl̩〕*adj.* 有教育意義的

fun〔fʌn〕*adj.* 有趣的

I like playing games. 　　　我喜歡玩遊戲。

They can be video games. 　　可能是電動遊戲。

They can be board games. 　　可能是棋盤遊戲。

I always try my best. 　　　我總是會盡全力。

There's no need to cheat! 　　不需要作弊！

Games are only fun if they are 　只有公平的遊戲才會有趣。
    fair.

It doesn't matter if I win or lose. 　我贏或輸都沒關係。

I always have a good time. 　　我總是玩得很愉快。

Games can bring me closer to 　　遊戲可以使我和朋友更
    my friends. 　　　　　　親密。

** ─────────────────

game〔gem〕*n.* 遊戲　　video〔'vɪdɪ,o〕*adj.* 影像的

video game 電動遊戲　　board〔bord〕*n.* (棋)盤

board game 棋盤遊戲　　*try one's best* 盡全力

cheat〔tʃit〕*v.* 作弊　　fair〔fɛr〕*adj.* 公平的

matter〔'mætə〕*v.* 有關係　　win〔wɪn〕*v.* 贏

lose〔luz〕*v.* 輸　　*have a good time* 玩得愉快

bring〔brɪŋ〕*v.* 使　　close〔klos〕*adj.* 親密的

close to 與…關係密切

I have many interests.	我有很多興趣。
My interests make life fun.	我的興趣使生活變得有趣。
I enjoy them very much.	我非常喜歡它們。
I know I can't always play.	我知道我不能一直玩樂。
Working hard is important.	努力用功很重要。
But sometimes I need to relax.	但有時候我需要放鬆。
We can find our own interests.	我們可以找到自己的興趣。
We can learn more about them.	我們可以更了解它們。
They can make life more	它們可以使生活變得更令人
exciting!	興奮！

**

life〔laɪf〕*n.* 生活
enjoy〔ɪn'dʒɔɪ〕*v.* 喜歡　　work〔wɝk〕*v.* 工作；用功
hard〔hɑrd〕*adv.* 努力地　　***work hard*** 努力用功
important〔ɪm'pɔrtn̩t〕*adj.* 重要的
relax〔rɪ'læks〕*v.* 放鬆　　find〔faɪnd〕*v.* 找到
learn〔lɝn〕*v.* 知道
exciting〔ɪk'saɪtɪŋ〕*adj.* 令人興奮的；刺激的

2

📋 背景說明

　　每個人感興趣的事物不一定相同，例如閱讀、寫作、跳舞等，但無論是靜態或動態的，它們都能讓你的生活更豐富。如果還不知道自己的興趣是什麼，試著多安排一些活動，也許就能找出自己的興趣所在，還能認識志趣相投的朋友。

1. *Today, **I would like to give a speech.***

   would like 想要（ = *want* ）

   speech〔 spitʃ 〕*n.* 演說　　***give a speech*** 發表演說

   　　would like 是作「想要」(= *want*) 解，所以這句話的意思是「今天，我想要發表演說。」也可說成：

   I'd like to tell you about it.

   （我想跟你們談論它。）

   I'd like to present my ideas.

   （我想說明我的想法。）

   I'd like to give a talk.

   （我想要演講。）

   present〔 prɪˋzɛnt 〕*v.* 提出

   idea〔 aɪˋdiə 〕*n.* 想法　　talk〔 tɔk 〕*n.* 演講

2. ***It can free my mind.***

free〔fri〕 *v.* 釋放　　mind〔maɪnd〕 *n.* 心靈；想法

　　　　free 主要是當形容詞用，作「自由的；免費的」解，在此是當動詞用，作「釋放」解。這句話的意思是「它可以釋放我的心靈。」也可說成：

It can open my mind.
（它可以讓我的心變得開闊。）

It can make me see things in a new way.
（它可以讓我用新的方式看事情。）

It can help me think in a new way.
（它可以幫我用新的方式來思考。）

【open〔'opən〕 *v.* 打開；使開闊　　way〔we〕 *n.* 方式】

3. ***It can open my heart.***

open〔'opən〕 *v.* 打開；使開闊　　heart〔hɑrt〕 *n.* 心

　　　　這句話的意思是「它可以使我的心胸變開闊。」也可說成：

It can release my feelings.
（它可以釋放我的情感。）

It can make me more compassionate.
（它可以讓我更有同情心。）

It can make me more tolerant.（它可以讓我更寬容。）

release〔rɪ'lis〕 *v.* 釋放　　feelings〔'filɪŋz〕 *n. pl.* 感情
compassionate〔kəm'pæʃənɪt〕 *adj.* 有同情心的
tolerant〔'tɑlərənt〕 *adj.* 寬容的

4. *I can dance to the beat*.

dance〔dæns〕*v.* 跳舞　　to〔tu〕*prep.* 隨著

beat〔bit〕*n.* 拍子

to 的基本意思是「向；到」，在此是作「隨著」解。

這句話的意思是「我會隨著節拍跳舞。」也可說成：

I can dance to the music.

（我會隨著音樂跳舞。）

I can dance to the rhythm.

（我會隨著節奏跳舞。）

I can dance in time to the music.

（我會合著音樂的節拍跳舞。）

【rhythm〔'rɪðəm〕*n.* 節奏　　*in time* 合節拍】

to 作「隨著」解，其用法舉例如下：

She sang *to* the accompaniment of the piano.

（她隨著鋼琴的伴奏唱歌。）

He tapped his foot *to* the beat of the song.

（他隨著歌曲的節拍輕輕地踏腳。）

accompaniment〔ə'kʌmpənɪmənt〕*n.* 伴奏

piano〔pɪ'æno〕*n.* 鋼琴

tap〔tæp〕*v.* 輕踏

5. ***I can sing along.***

along〔 ə'lɔŋ 〕 *adv.* 一起

這句話的意思是「我會一起唱歌。」也可說成：

I can sing, too.（我也會唱歌。）

I can sing with the singers.
（我會和那些歌手一起唱。）

I can sing while the music plays.
（我會在播放音樂的時候唱歌。）

singer〔'sɪŋɚ 〕 *n.* 歌手
while〔 hwaɪl 〕 *conj.* 當…的時候　　play〔 ple 〕 *v.* 播放

　　along 當介系詞用時，是作「沿著」解，在此是當副詞用，作「一起」解，而和 with 連用時，則作「連同」解，其用法舉例如下：

We're going to the movies — do you want to
　come ***along***?
（我們要去看電影——你想一起來嗎？）

Joe came to the party ***along with*** his sister Sue.
（喬和他的妹妹蘇一起來參加派對。）

I brought two pairs of shorts ***along with*** two
　T-shirts.（我帶了兩件短褲和兩件 T 恤。）

go to the movies 去看電影　　party〔'pɑrtɪ 〕 *n.* 派對
along with 連同　　shorts〔 ʃɔrts 〕 *n. pl.* 短褲
a pair of shorts 一條短褲　　T-shirt〔'ti,ʃɜt 〕 *n.* T 恤

6. ***Music puts me in a good mood.***

put〔put〕*v.* 使處於（某種狀態）

mood〔mud〕*n.* 心情　　***in a good mood*** 心情好

　　　這句話字面的意思是「音樂把我放在好的心情裡面。」
引申為「音樂使我心情很好。」也可說成：

Music makes me happy.
（音樂使我快樂。）

Music makes me feel good.
（音樂使我心情好。）

Music improves my mood.
（音樂使我的心情變好。）

【improve〔ɪm'pruv〕*v.* 改善】

in a ~ mood 用來表示「心情 ~」，其用法舉例如下：

Watch out! Joan is ***in a bad mood*** today.
（小心！瓊今天心情不好。）

Gloria was ***in a melancholy mood*** and sat
　watching sad movies all day.
（葛洛麗雅心情憂鬱，一整天都坐著看悲傷的電影。）

Grandpa's stories put us all ***in a nostalgic mood***.
（祖父的故事使我們處於懷舊的氣氛中。）

Watch out! 小心！
melancholy〔'mɛlən‚kɑlɪ〕*adj.* 憂鬱的
grandpa〔'grændpɑ〕*n.* 祖父　　story〔'storɪ〕*n.* 故事
nostalgic〔nɑ'stældʒɪk〕*adj.* 懷舊的

7. *The actors are larger-than-life!*

actor〔ˈæktɚ〕*n.* 演員

larger-than-life〔ˈlɑrdʒɚðənˈlaɪf〕*adj.* 令人印象極深刻的；
有英雄色彩的

life 可作「實物」解，larger-than-life 字面的意思
是「比實際的人或物誇大」，引申為「令人印象極深刻的；
有英雄色彩的」，所以這句話的意思是「演員都令人印象
極深刻！」或「演員都充滿英雄色彩！」也可說成：

The actors are heroic.
（演員都很英勇。）

The actors are impressive.
（演員都令人印象深刻。）

The actors are more interesting and exciting
than ordinary people.
（演員比一般人更有趣，而且更令人興奮。）

heroic〔hɪˈro‧ɪk〕*adj.* 英勇的

impressive〔ɪmˈprɛsɪv〕*adj.* 令人印象深刻的

interesting〔ˈɪntrɪstɪŋ〕*adj.* 有趣的

exciting〔ɪkˈsaɪtɪŋ〕*adj.* 令人興奮的

ordinary〔ˈɔrdṇˌɛrɪ〕*adj.* 普通的；一般的

8. *I always try my best.*

try one's *best* 盡全力

　　best 在這裡不是作「最棒的」解，而是作「最大的努力」解，所以這句話的意思是「我總是會盡全力。」也可說成：

> I always do the best I can.
> （我總是會盡自己最大的努力。）
>
> I always try my hardest.
> （我總是會盡自己最大的努力。）
>
> I always make my best effort.
> （我總是會盡自己最大的努力。）
>
> *do the best* one *can* 盡自己最大的努力
> *try* one's *hardest* 盡自己最大的努力
> effort〔ˈɛfət〕*n.* 努力
> *make* one's *best effort* 盡自己最大的努力

9. *Games can bring me closer to my friends.*

bring〔brɪŋ〕*v.* 使
close〔klos〕*adj.* 親近的；親密的
close to 與…關係密切

　　這句話的意思是「遊戲可以使我跟朋友的關係更密切。」也可說成：

Games can make people feel closer.

（遊戲可以使人覺得更親近。）

Playing games can increase our feelings
　of affection.

（玩遊戲可以增加我們的感情。）

Games can make friends more intimate.

（遊戲可以使朋友更親密。）

increase〔ɪnˈkris〕*v.* 增加
affection〔əˈfɛkʃən〕*n.* 感情
intimate〔ˈɪntəmɪt〕*adj.* 親密的

10. *We can learn more about them.*

learn〔lɝn〕*v.* 知道

　　learn 的基本意思是「學習」，在此是作「知道」
解。這句話的意思是「我們可以更了解它們。」也可
說成：

We can find out more about them.

（我們可以發現更多和它們相關的事。）

We can explore them.

（我們可以探索它們。）

We can research them.

（我們可以研究它們。）

find out 發現　　explore〔ɪkˈsplor〕*v.* 探索
research〔rɪˈsɝtʃ〕*v.* 研究

 作文範例

My Interests

Work is important, but we cannot work all the time. We need to develop some outside interests in order to live well. They will add not only variety but also fun to our lives. They will help us to live in a more balanced way.

I have several interests that I pursue in my free time. Among them, I really like music because it can free my mind and open my heart. Music always puts me in a good mood. I also enjoy movies. I like all kinds of movies, including comedies, action movies, and romances. *In addition*, I read a lot. Books take me to another world and are also educational. They make learning fun. *Finally*, I like playing games, not only video games but board games and card games, too. It's a way for my friends and I to get closer.

I am lucky to have many interests. After spending some time doing one of the things I like, I return to work refreshed and energized.

📖 中文翻譯

我的興趣

　　用功很重要，但我們不可能一直都在用功。我們需要培養一些課餘的興趣，以便能好好地過生活。它們不但能使生活增加變化，還能增添樂趣。它們能幫助我們以更均衡的方式過生活。

　　我有幾個興趣，是我在空閒時間會去從事的。在這些興趣當中，我真的很喜歡音樂，因為它可以釋放我的心靈，並開闊我的心胸。音樂總是讓我心情很好。我也喜歡電影。我喜歡各種電影，包括喜劇片、動作片，和愛情片。此外，我常常看書。書能帶領我到另一個世界，同時還有教育意義。書能讓學習變得有趣。最後，我喜歡玩遊戲，不只是電動玩具，還有棋盤遊戲和紙牌遊戲。這是一個能讓我與朋友更親近的方法。

　　我很幸運能擁有很多興趣。花些時間做我喜歡的事情之後，我便能神清氣爽且精力充沛地回來用功。

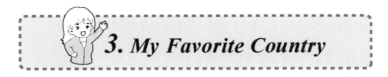

3. My Favorite Country

Welcome, ladies and gentlemen.
It's nice to see all of you.
I hope you are all feeling great.

My speech today is about a place.
It's a place that is very special to me.
It's a place that is close to my heart.

I would like to tell you about my
    favorite country.
It is located just north of the USA.
My favorite country is Canada.

---

favorite〔'fevərɪt〕   country〔'kʌntrɪ〕
nice〔naɪs〕   hope〔hop〕
feel〔fil〕   great〔gret〕
speech〔spitʃ〕   *be close to one's heart*
locate〔'loket , lo'ket〕   north〔nɔrθ〕
the USA   Canada〔'kænədə〕

Canada is a very clean country.

It has a lot of fresh air.

It has a lot of clean water.

There are many famous parks.

There are a lot of large mountains.

Canada is known for its scenery.

Canadians try to keep Canada beautiful.

They like to keep things clean.

Canadians care about their environment.

---

clean ﹝ klin ﹞   *a lot of*

fresh ﹝ frɛʃ ﹞   air ﹝ ɛr ﹞

famous ﹝'feməs ﹞   mountain ﹝'maʊntn̩ ﹞

known ﹝ non ﹞   *be known for*

scenery ﹝'sinərɪ ﹞   Canadian ﹝ kə'nedɪən ﹞

try ﹝ traɪ ﹞   keep ﹝ kip ﹞

care about

environment ﹝ ɪn'vaɪrənmənt ﹞

Canada is also very multicultural.

Many different kinds of people live there.

Everyone lives in peace.

It doesn't matter where they are from.

It doesn't matter how they grew up.

They live together all the same.

3

Going to Canada is special.

We don't just get to see one country.

We can see almost the whole world.

---

multicultural (ˌmʌltɪ'kʌltʃərəl , ˌmʌltaɪ-)

different ('dɪfrənt)   kind (kaɪnd)

peace (pis)   *in peace*

matter ('mætɚ)   *grow up*

all the same   *get to*

almost ('ɔlˌmost)   whole (hol)

world (wɝld)

***Canadians are also very polite**.*

***They are** well-mannered.*

***They are** really friendly.*

Canadians often say "please" and "thanks".

Canadians like to help strangers.

Canadians don't like to curse.

Good manners make life more pleasant.

Canada is famous for this.

It's a very nice place to be.

---

polite〔pə'laɪt〕

well-mannered〔'wɛl'mænəd〕

really〔'rɪəlɪ〕   friendly〔'frɛndlɪ〕

stranger〔'strendʒə〕   curse〔kɝs〕

manners〔'mænəz〕   life〔laɪf〕

pleasant〔'plɛznt〕   *be famous for*

be〔bi〕

3

Finally*, *Canada is a ton of fun!

There's always something to do there.

We'll never get bored.

We can go bike riding in the spring.

We can go swimming in the summer.

We can go skiing in the winter.

The leaves even turn orange in the fall.

It's very pretty!

Canada is a beautiful place.

---

finally (ˈfaɪnl̩ɪ)	***a ton of***
fun (fʌn)	get (gɛt)
bored (bord)	bike (baɪk)
ride (raɪd)	spring (sprɪŋ)
swim (swɪm)	summer (ˈsʌmɚ)
ski (ski)	winter (ˈwɪntɚ)
leaves (livz)	even (ˈivən)
turn (tɜn)	orange (ˈɔrɪndʒ)
fall (fɔl)	pretty (ˈprɪtɪ)

I think Canada is a great place to live.

Its scenery is unique.

Its people are very kind.

I love Taiwan.

It will always be my home.

But I think Canada is wonderful.

Traveling can be a lot of fun.

Canada is a perfect place for a
vacation.

I hope I can go to Canada soon!

---

unique〔ju'nik〕   kind〔kaɪnd〕

wonderful〔'wʌndɚfəl〕   traveling〔'trævḷɪŋ〕

perfect〔'pɝfɪkt〕   vacation〔ve'keʃən〕

soon〔sun〕

3. **My Favorite Country**

🔊 演講解說

3

***Welcome**, **ladies and gentlemen**.*	歡迎各位先生，各位女士。
***It's nice to see all of you**.*	非常高興看到你們。
***I hope you are all feeling great**.*	希望你們心情都很好。
My speech today is about a place.	我今天的演講是關於一個地方。
It's a place that is very special to me.	它對我來說是個很特別的地方。
It's a place that is close to my heart.	它是我非常關心的地方。
I would like to tell you about my favorite country.	我想告訴你們我最喜愛的國家。
It is located just north of the USA.	它就位於美國的北方。
My favorite country is Canada.	我最喜愛的國家是加拿大。

** ————

favorite〔'fevərɪt〕*adj.* 最喜愛的　country〔'kʌntrɪ〕*n.* 國家
nice〔naɪs〕*adj.* 愉快的　hope〔hop〕*v.* 希望
speech〔spitʃ〕*n.* 演講　***be close to** one's **heart*** 某人非常關心的
locate〔'loket , lo'ket〕*v.* 使位於　north〔nɔrθ〕*adv.* 在北方
the USA 美國　Canada〔'kænədə〕*n.* 加拿大

Canada is a very clean country.	加拿大是一個很乾淨的國家。
It has a lot of fresh air.	它有很多新鮮的空氣。
It has a lot of clean water.	它有很多無污染的水。
There are many famous parks.	有很多有名的公園。
There are a lot of large mountains.	有很多高山。
Canada is known for its scenery.	加拿大因風景而聞名。
Canadians try to keep Canada beautiful.	加拿大人努力讓加拿大保持美麗。
They like to keep things clean.	他們喜歡讓東西保持乾淨。
Canadians care about their environment.	加拿大人關心他們的環境。

** ─────────────────

clean〔klin〕*adj.* 乾淨的；未受污染的　　*a lot of* 許多
fresh〔frɛʃ〕*adj.* 新鮮的　　air〔ɛr〕*n.* 空氣
famous〔'feməs〕*adj.* 有名的　　mountain〔'mauntṇ〕*n.* 山
known〔non〕*adj.* 聞名的　　*be known for* 因…而聞名
scenery〔'sinərɪ〕*n.* 風景　　Canadian〔kə'nedɪən〕*n.* 加拿大人
try〔traɪ〕*v.* 嘗試；努力　　keep〔kip〕*v.* 使維持（某種狀態）
care about 關心　　environment〔ɪn'vaɪrənmənt〕*n.* 環境

3

Canada is also very multicultural. 加拿大也融合了多種文化。

Many different kinds of people 很多不同種類的人住在

　　live there. 那裡。

Everyone lives in peace. 每個人都和睦相處。

It doesn't matter where they 他們來自何方並不重要。

　　are from.

It doesn't matter how they grew up. 他們如何成長並不重要。

They live together all the same. 他們照樣生活在一起。

Going to Canada is special. 去加拿大很特別。

We don't just get to see one country. 我們不只能看見一個國家。

We can see almost the whole world. 我們幾乎可以看見全世界。

** ————————————————

multicultural〔͵mʌltɪˈkʌltʃərəl ,͵mʌltaɪ-〕*adj.* 融合多種文化的

different〔ˈdɪfrənt〕*adj.* 不同的

kind〔kaɪnd〕*n.* 種類　　peace〔pis〕*n.* 和平；和睦

in peace 安靜地；和睦地

matter〔ˈmætɚ〕*v.* 有關係；重要　　*grow up* 成長

all the same 仍然；照樣　　*get to* 得以；能夠

almost〔ˈɔl͵most〕*adv.* 幾乎　　whole〔hol〕*adj.* 全部的

world〔wɝld〕*n.* 世界

Canadians are also very polite.	加拿大人也很客氣。
They are well-mannered.	他們很有禮貌。
They are really friendly.	他們真的很友善。
Canadians often say "please" and "thanks".	加拿大人常常說「請」和「謝謝」。
Canadians like to help strangers.	加拿大人喜歡幫助陌生人。
Canadians don't like to curse.	加拿大人不喜歡咒罵。
Good manners make life more pleasant.	有禮貌能使生活變得更令人愉快。
Canada is famous for this.	加拿大因此而聞名。
It's a very nice place to be.	它是一個可以停留的好地方。

** ————————————————

polite〔 pəˋlaɪt 〕*adj.* 有禮貌的；客氣的
well-mannered〔ˋwɛlˋmænəd 〕*adj.* 有禮貌的；態度良好的
really〔ˋrɪəlɪ 〕*adv.* 真地　　friendly〔ˋfrɛndlɪ 〕*adj.* 友善的
stranger〔ˋstrendʒə 〕*n.* 陌生人　　curse〔 kɝs 〕*v.* 咒罵
manners〔ˋmænəz 〕*n. pl.* 禮貌　　life〔 laɪf 〕*n.* 生活
pleasant〔ˋplɛzn̩t 〕*adj.* 令人愉快的
be famous for 因…而聞名（ *= be known for* ）
be〔 bi 〕*v.* 逗留；待

Finally*, *Canada is a ton of fun!　　　最後，加拿大很有趣！

There's always something to do　　　那裡總是有事情可以做。
　　there.

We'll never get bored.　　　我們絕不會感到無聊。

We can go bike riding in the　　　我們可以在春天騎腳踏車。
　　spring.

We can go swimming in the　　　我們可以在夏天游泳。
　　summer.

We can go skiing in the winter.　　　我們可以在冬天滑雪。

The leaves even turn orange in　　　甚至樹葉會在秋天變成橘
　　the fall.　　　色的。

It's very pretty!　　　非常漂亮！

Canada is a beautiful place.　　　加拿大是一個美麗的地方。

3

** ————————————————

finally〔ˈfaɪnḷɪ〕*adv.* 最後　　***a ton of*** 許多

fun〔fʌn〕*n.* 樂趣　　get〔gɛt〕*v.* 變得

bored〔bord〕*adj.* 無聊的　　bike〔baɪk〕*n.* 腳踏車

ride〔raɪd〕*v.* 騎　　spring〔sprɪŋ〕*n.* 春天

swim〔swɪm〕*v.* 游泳　　summer〔ˈsʌmɚ〕*n.* 夏天

ski〔ski〕*v.* 滑雪　　winter〔ˈwɪntɚ〕*n.* 冬天

leaves〔livz〕*n. pl.* 葉子【單數是 leaf】　　even〔ˈivən〕*adv.* 甚至

turn〔tɝn〕*v.* 變成　　orange〔ˈɔrɪndʒ〕*adj.* 橘色的

fall〔fɔl〕*n.* 秋天　　pretty〔ˈprɪtɪ〕*adj.* 漂亮的

I think Canada is a great place to live.	我認為加拿大是一個可以居住的好地方。
Its scenery is unique.	它的風景很獨特。
Its people are very kind.	它的人民很親切。
I love Taiwan.	我愛台灣。
It will always be my home.	它將永遠是我的家。
But I think Canada is wonderful.	但我覺得加拿大眞是太棒了。
Traveling can be a lot of fun.	旅行可以是很有趣的。
Canada is a perfect place for a vacation.	加拿大是一個度假的完美地點。
I hope I can go to Canada soon!	希望我很快就可以去加拿大！

** ————————————————

unique〔ju`nik〕*adj.* 獨特的
kind〔kaɪnd〕*adj.* 親切的
wonderful〔`wʌndəfəl〕*adj.* 極好的；很棒的
traveling〔`trævḷɪŋ〕*n.* 旅行
perfect〔`pɝfɪkt〕*adj.* 完美的
vacation〔ve`keʃən〕*n.* 假期
soon〔sun〕*adv.* 不久；很快

📖 背景說明

　　環遊世界幾乎是每個人的夢想，但並非每個人都有足夠的時間與金錢去完成它。試著回想你過去旅遊的經驗，或是看過的旅遊資訊介紹，在這麼多國家中，你最喜愛哪一個國家？試著用英文向大家介紹它。

3

1. ***It's a place that is close to my heart****.*

   be close to *one's* ***heart*** 某人非常關心

   　　be close to *one's* ***heart*** 字面的意思是「很接近某人的心」，引申為「某人非常關心」。這句話的意思是「它是我非常關心的地方。」也可說成：

   > It's a country that is very dear to me.
   > （它是我心愛的國家。）

   > It's a place that I care a lot about.
   > （它是我很關心的地方。）

   > It's a place that is very special to me.
   > （它對我來說是很特別的地方。）

   country〔ˈkʌntrɪ〕*n.* 國家
   dear〔dɪr〕*adj.* 心愛的；珍視的
   care about 關心　　***a lot*** 很
   special〔ˈspɛʃəl〕*adj.* 特別的

2. ***It is located just north of the USA.***

   locate〔'loket , lo'ket〕*v.* 使位於

   north〔nɔrθ〕*adv.* 在北方　　***the USA*** 美國

   　　　locate 這個動詞，如果表「位於～」，常用被動
   語態。這句話的意思是「它就位於美國的北方。」也
   可說成：

   > It's just north of the U.S.
   > （它就在美國的北方。）
   >
   > It lies just north of the United States.
   > （它就位於美國的北方。）
   >
   > It's to the north of the USA.
   > （它在美國以北。）
   >
   > ***the U.S.*** 美國（= *the United States*
   > 　　= *the USA* = *America*）
   > lie〔laɪ〕*v.* 位於
   > ***to the north of*** 在～以北

3. ***Canada is known for its scenery.***

   known〔non〕*adj.* 聞名的

   be known for 因…而聞名

   scenery〔'sinərɪ〕*n.* 風景

   　　這句話的意思是「加拿大因風景
   而聞名。」也可說成：

3

Canada's scenery is renowned.
（加拿大的風景很有名。）

Canada is famous for its scenery.
（加拿大因風景而聞名。）

Canada is celebrated for its beautiful vistas.
（加拿大以美麗的景色而聞名。）

renowned〔rɪ'naʊnd〕*adj.* 有名的
famous〔'feməs〕*adj.* 有名的
be famous for 因…而聞名
celebrated〔'sɛlə,bretɪd〕*adj.* 有名的
be celebrated for 以…而聞名　　vista〔'vɪstə〕*n.* 景色

4. *Canada is also very multicultural.*
multicultural〔,mʌltɪ'kʌltʃərəl , ,mʌltaɪ-〕*adj.* 融合多種文化的

這句話的意思是「加拿大也融合了多種文化。」
也可説成：

The population of Canada consists of people
　from a variety of cultures.
（加拿大的居民是由來自各種文化的人所組成。）

People from all over the world have settled in
　Canada.（來自世界各地的人定居於加拿大。）

The people of Canada have a wide variety
　of backgrounds.
（加拿大的居民有很多各式各樣的背景。）

population〔͵pɑpjəˈleʃən〕 *n.* 人口；居民

consist of 由～組成　　***a variety of*** 各種的

culture〔ˈkʌltʃɚ〕 *n.* 文化　　***all over the world*** 全世界

settle〔ˈsɛtḷ〕 *v.* 定居 *< in >*

wide〔waɪd〕 *adj.* （範圍）廣泛的

a wide variety of 很多各式各樣的

background〔ˈbæk͵graʊnd〕 *n.* 背景

另外，multi- 是表「多…」的字首，例如：

This is a ***multi***national company.

（這是一間跨國公司。）

The ***multi***colored jacket is

　certainly unusual.

（這件彩色的夾克一定很少見。）

multinational〔͵mʌltɪˈnæʃənḷ〕 *adj.* 多國的；跨國的

multicolored〔͵mʌltɪˈkʌlɚd〕 *adj.* 多色的；彩色的

jacket〔ˈdʒækɪt〕 *n.* 夾克

certainly〔ˈsɝtṇlɪ〕 *adv.* 一定

unusual〔ʌnˈjuʒʊəl〕 *adj.* 不尋常的；罕見的

5. ***Everyone lives in peace.***

peace〔pis〕 *n.* 和平；和睦

in peace 安靜地；和睦地

　　這句話字面的意思是「每個人都住在和平之中。」
引申爲「每個人都和睦相處。」也可説成：

Everyone gets along. (每個人都處得很好。)

Everyone lives peacefully.

(每個人都和睦相處。)

There is no discord. (沒有衝突。)

get along 相處；處得好

peacefully 〔'pisfəlɪ〕 *adv.* 和平地

discord 〔'dɪskɔrd〕 *n.* 不和；衝突

6. *They live together all the same.*

　all the same 仍然；照樣

　　all the same 字面的意思是「全都一樣」，引申為「仍然；照樣」。這句話的意思是「他們照樣生活在一起。」也可說成：

They live together anyway.

(他們還是生活在一起。)

They live together regardless.

(不管怎樣，他們生活在一起。)

They get along despite their differences.

(雖然他們有差異，他們卻能處得很好。)

anyway 〔'ɛnɪ,we〕 *adv.* 無論如何；還是

regardless 〔rɪ'gɑrdlɪs〕 *adv.* 不顧一切地；不管怎樣

despite 〔dɪ'spaɪt〕 *prep.* 雖然

difference 〔'dɪfrəns〕 *n.* 不同；差異

7. ***We don't just get to see one country.***

   get to 得以；能夠

   　　　　這句話的意思是「我們不只能看見一個國家。」
   也可說成：

   We don't see just Canada.
   （我們不會只看見加拿大。）

   We don't see just one nation.
   （我們不會只看見一個國家。）

   We get to experience more than one country.
   （我們能體驗到一個以上的國家。）

   nation〔'neʃən〕*n.* 國家
   experience〔ɪk'spɪrɪəns〕*v.* 體驗

8. ***They are well-mannered.***

   well-mannered〔'wɛl'mænəd〕*adj.* 有禮貌的；態度良好的

   　　　　well- 是表「良好；充分」的複合用詞，例如
   well-known（有名的）、well-dressed（穿著體面的）
   等，而 well-mannered 則作「有禮貌的；態度良好的」
   解。這句話的意思是「他們很有禮貌。」也可說成：

   They are courteous.（他們很有禮貌。）
   They are polite.（他們很有禮貌。）
   They are civil.（他們很有禮貌。）

   courteous〔'kɝtɪəs〕*adj.* 有禮貌的
   polite〔pə'laɪt〕*adj.* 有禮貌的　　civil〔'sɪvl̩〕*adj.* 有禮貌的

9. *Canadians don't like to curse.*

curse〔kɝs〕*v.* 咒罵

這句話的意思是「加拿大人不喜歡咒罵。」也可
說成：

Canadians don't like to swear.
（加拿大人不喜歡咒罵。）

Canadians don't use four-letter words.
（加拿大人不會使用粗俗不雅的字。）

Canadians don't use foul language.
（加拿大人不說下流話。）

swear〔swɛr〕*v.* 發誓；咒罵
four-letter word 粗俗不雅的字（由四個字母構成的
單音節的詞，例如 fuck、shit 等）
foul〔faʊl〕*adj.* 下流的
language〔ˈlæŋgwɪdʒ〕*n.* 語言；言詞

10. *Finally, Canada is a ton of fun!*

finally〔ˈfaɪnḷɪ〕*adv.* 最後　　***a ton of*** 許多
fun〔fʌn〕*n.* 樂趣

ton 的基本意思是「噸」，a ton of fun 字面的意思
是「一噸的樂趣」，引申為「許多樂趣」，所以這句話的
意思是「最後，加拿大很有趣！」也可說成：

Lastly, Canada is a lot of fun!

（最後，加拿大很有趣！）

We can have a great time in Canada!

（我們在加拿大可以玩得很愉快！）

Finally, there's a lot to enjoy in Canada!

（最後，在加拿大有很多事物可以享受！）

lastly〔'læstlɪ〕adv. 最後

have a great time 玩得很愉快

enjoy〔ɪn'dʒɔɪ〕v. 享受

11. *Canada is a perfect place for a vacation.*

perfect〔'pɝfɪkt〕adj. 完美的

vacation〔ve'keʃən〕n. 假期

　　這句話的意思是「加拿大是一個度假的完美地點。」
也可說成：

Canada is a wonderful place to visit.

（加拿大是一個遊覽的好地方。）

Canada is an ideal place for a holiday.

（加拿大是一個度假的理想地方。）

wonderful〔'wʌndəfəl〕adj. 極好的

ideal〔aɪ'diəl〕adj. 理想的

holiday〔'hɑlə,de〕n. 假期

 作文範例

My Favorite Country

There is one place in the world that is very special to me. It's a country of great beauty and culture. Although I am not a native of it, Canada is my favorite country.

There are several reasons why I am so fond of Canada. *For one thing*, it is a very clean country with beautiful scenery. Canadians care about their environment and work hard to keep it unpolluted. Another reason that I like Canada is that it is multicultural. Many different kinds of people live in Canada, yet they all get along. A visit there is like a trip around the world. *Moreover*, Canadians are generally very polite. They often say "please" and "thank you", and they like to help strangers. *Finally*, Canada is fun. There are so many things to do and see there. Visitors can try cycling or skiing, or simply marvel at the fall colors.

In short, Canada is a great place. The people are kind and the natural environment is lovely. Canada is not my home, but it is a place I am sure to return to again and again.

3

中文翻譯

我最喜愛的國家

在這世界上有一個地方對我而言是非常特別的。那是一個非常美麗又有文化的國家。雖然我不是在那裡出生，但加拿大是我最喜愛的國家。

我這麼喜歡加拿大的理由有幾個。首先，它是一個風景美麗又乾淨的國家。加拿大人很關心自己的環境，並努力保護它不受污染。另外一個我喜歡加拿大的理由是，那裡融合了多種文化。很多不同種類的人居住在加拿大，但是他們都能相處得很好。去那裡遊覽就像是一趟環遊世界之旅。此外，加拿大的人普遍都非常有禮貌。他們常說「請」和「謝謝」，而且他們喜歡幫助陌生人。最後，加拿大很有趣。那裡有很多事物可以做和參觀。觀光客可以嘗試騎腳踏車或滑雪，或只是對秋天的色彩感到驚嘆。

總之，加拿大是一個很棒的地方。人民很親切，而且自然環境很漂亮。加拿大不是我的祖國，但它是一個我一定會一再回去的地方。

4. My Favorite Song

You all have arrived very quickly!
We will begin soon.
Thank you for coming.

My favorite song is marvelous.
It is a major part of my life.
Sometimes I hear it in my dreams.

This song brings back memories.
I can express myself with it.
Here are some more things about it.

arrive〔ə'raɪv〕	quickly〔'kwɪklɪ〕
begin〔bɪ'gɪn〕	soon〔sun〕
marvelous〔'marvḷəs〕	major〔'medʒɚ〕
life〔laɪf〕	sometimes〔'sʌm,taɪmz〕
hear〔hɪr〕	dream〔drim〕
bring back	memory〔'mɛmərɪ〕
express〔ɪk'sprɛs〕	myself〔maɪ'sɛlf〕

The song is about me.

I heard it once on the radio.

The words spoke to me.

After hearing it, I felt strong.

It lifted me up when I was down.

I listened to it before a test in school.

Now I listen to it in the morning

   on the MRT.

It helps me think and wake up.

I love to sing along to it.

---

once 〔 wʌns 〕	radio 〔'redɪˌo 〕
words 〔 wɝdz 〕	***speak to***
strong 〔 strɔŋ 〕	lift 〔 lɪft 〕
lift sb. up	down 〔 daʊn 〕
listen 〔'lɪsn̩ 〕	test 〔 tɛst 〕
MRT	help 〔 hɛlp 〕
think 〔 θɪŋk 〕	***wake up***
along 〔 ə'lɔŋ 〕	***sing along to~***

It is also a song to exercise to.

Frankly, its beat is the best!

It helps me push through difficult parts.

At the end I have the courage to finish.

My power is greater.

I feel fantastic!

Some people do not like it.

They say it gives them a headache.

But I think it helps me.

4

---

exercise（'ɛksɚ͵saɪz）   frankly（'fræŋklɪ）

beat（bit）   ***push through***

difficult（'dɪfə͵kʌlt）   part（pɑrt）

at the end   courage（'kɝɪdʒ）

finish（'fɪnɪʃ）   power（'pauɚ）

great（gret）   fantastic（fæn'tæstɪk）

headache（'hɛd͵ek）

***Also, its tune is easy to remember*.**

I can sing it all day long.

My voice is not the best.

My friends sometimes tell me to stop.

But I keep going.

It is impolite, but humorous, too.

Sometimes, my friends sing along
 with me.

I tell them the words.

They do not always sing them correctly.

---

also (′ɔlso)   tune (tjun)

easy (′izɪ)   remember (rɪ′mɛmbɚ)

all day long   voice (vɔɪs)

stop (stɑp)   keep (kip)

keep going   impolite (ˌɪmpə′laɪt)

humorous (′hjumərəs)   ***sing along with*** *sb.*

not always   correctly (kə′rɛktlɪ)

Finally, *my song brings memories*.

I remember when I was younger.

Those were happy times.

I realize how lucky I am to
  be alive.

I hear the music and regret nothing.

It is easier to be me.

4

Some bad memories come up.

But my song makes them better.

It pushes the bad ones out.

---

finally (ˈfaɪnḷɪ)   bring (brɪŋ)
young (jʌŋ)   realize (ˈrɪəˌlaɪz)
lucky (ˈlʌkɪ)   alive (əˈlaɪv)
regret (rɪˈgrɛt)   *come up*
push out

It is good to have a favorite song.

You will become stronger and
　happier.

Listen closely and it will come.

It must have a melody.

The rhythm is important, too.

Most important are the words.

My favorite song helps me.

I think everyone should have one.

They always mean a lot!

become ﹝ bɪˋkʌm ﹞　　　closely ﹝ˋkloslɪ ﹞

come ﹝ kʌm ﹞　　　　melody ﹝ˋmɛlədɪ ﹞

rhythm ﹝ˋrɪðəm ﹞　　　important ﹝ ɪmˋpɔrtn̩t ﹞

mean ﹝ min ﹞　　　　*mean a lot*

4. My Favorite Song

🔊 演講解說

You all have arrived very quickly!	你們都很快就到了！
We will begin soon.	我們很快就要開始了。
Thank you for coming.	謝謝你們的到來。
My favorite song is marvelous.	我最喜愛的歌曲是很棒的。
It is a major part of my life.	它是我生活中較重要的部分。
Sometimes I hear it in my dreams.	有時我會在夢裡聽見它。
This song brings back memories.	這首歌使我想起往事。
I can express myself with it.	我可以用它來表達自己。
Here are some more things about it.	以下是更多關於它的事。

4

** ————————————

arrive〔əˋraɪv〕v. 到達　　quickly〔ˋkwɪklɪ〕adv. 快速地

begin〔bɪˋgɪn〕v. 開始　　soon〔sun〕adv. 不久；很快

marvelous〔ˋmɑrvḷəs〕adj. 令人驚嘆的；很棒的

major〔ˋmedʒɚ〕adj. 主要的；較重要的　　life〔laɪf〕n. 生活

sometimes〔ˋsʌmˏtaɪmz〕adv. 有時候　　hear〔hɪr〕v. 聽見

dream〔drim〕n. 夢　　***bring back*** 使人想起

memory〔ˋmɛmərɪ〕n. 回憶　　express〔ɪkˋsprɛs〕v. 表達

myself〔maɪˋsɛlf〕pron. 我自己

The song is about me.	這首歌就是在說我。
I heard it once on the radio.	我以前在廣播聽過一次。
The words spoke to me.	歌詞打動我的心。
After hearing it, I felt strong.	聽完後，我覺得更堅強。
It lifted me up when I was down.	當我情緒低落時，它能使我振作。
I listened to it before a test in school.	在學校考試前，我會聽這首歌。
Now I listen to it in the morning on the MRT.	現在我早上會在捷運上聽這首歌。
It helps me think and wake up.	它能幫助我思考和清醒。
I love to sing along to it.	我喜歡跟著它一起唱。

** ─────────────────────

once〔wʌns〕*adv.* 一次　　radio〔ˋredɪˏo〕*n.* 收音機；無線電廣播
words〔wɝdz〕*n. pl.* 歌詞　　**speak to** 動（人）心弦
strong〔strɔŋ〕*adj.* 強壯的；堅強的　　lift〔lɪft〕*v.* 使振作
lift sb. up 使某人振作　　down〔daʊn〕*adj.* 情緒低落的
listen〔ˋlɪsn̩〕*v.* 傾聽　　test〔tɛst〕*n.* 測驗
MRT 捷運（= mass rapid transit）
help〔hɛlp〕*v.* 幫助；有助於　　think〔θɪŋk〕*v.* 想；思考
wake up 醒來；清醒　　along〔əˋlɔŋ〕*adv.* 一起
sing along to~ 配合著~一起唱

It is also a song to exercise to.	它也是運動時可以聽的歌。
Frankly, its beat is the best!	坦白說，它的節拍是最棒的！
It helps me push through difficult parts.	它幫助我完成困難的部分。
At the end I have the courage to finish.	最後我能有勇氣做完。
My power is greater.	我的力量變得強大了。
I feel fantastic!	我覺得棒極了！
Some people do not like it.	有些人不喜歡它。
They say it gives them a headache.	他們說這首歌會讓他們頭痛。
But I think it helps me.	但我認為它對我有幫助。

4

** ——————————————

exercise〔ˈɛksəˌsaɪz〕v. 運動
frankly〔ˈfræŋklɪ〕adv. 坦白說　　beat〔bit〕n. 節拍
push through 設法完成　　difficult〔ˈdɪfəˌkʌlt〕adj. 困難的
part〔pɑrt〕n. 部分　　*at the end* 最後
courage〔ˈkɝɪdʒ〕n. 勇氣　　finish〔ˈfɪnɪʃ〕v. 完成
power〔ˈpaʊə〕n. 力量　　great〔gret〕adj. 大的
fantastic〔fænˈtæstɪk〕adj. 很棒的
headache〔ˈhɛdˌek〕n. 頭痛

Also**, **its tune is easy to remember.　而且，它的旋律很好記。

I can sing it all day long.　我可以唱這首歌唱一整天。

My voice is not the best.　我的歌聲不是最好的。

My friends sometimes tell me
　to stop.　我的朋友有時會叫我停止。

But I keep going.　但是我會持續地唱。

It is impolite, but humorous, too.　這樣很不禮貌，但也很好笑。

Sometimes, my friends sing
　along with me.　有時候，我的朋友會跟我
一起唱。

I tell them the words.　我告訴他們歌詞。

They do not always sing them
　correctly.　他們不一定唱得對。

**　*

also〔ˋɔlso〕*adv.* 而且　　tune〔tjun〕*n.* 旋律

easy〔ˋizɪ〕*adj.* 容易的　　remember〔rɪˋmɛmbɚ〕*v.* 記得

all day long 整天　　voice〔vɔɪs〕*n.* 聲音

stop〔stɑp〕*v.* 停止　　keep〔kip〕*v.* 持續

keep going 持續進行　　impolite〔͵ɪmpəˋlaɪt〕*adj.* 不禮貌的

humorous〔ˋhjumərəs〕*adj.* 幽默的；好笑的

sing along with *sb.* 和某人一起唱

not always 不一定；未必

correctly〔kəˋrɛktlɪ〕*adv.* 正確地

Finally, my song brings memories.	最後，我的歌能勾起回憶。
I remember when I was younger.	我想起我年幼的時候。
Those were happy times.	那些都是快樂的時光。
I realize how lucky I am to be alive.	我了解到我能活著是多麼的幸運。
I hear the music and regret nothing.	我聽見這個音樂，就不會對任何事情感到後悔。
It is easier to be me.	做自己會比較容易。
Some bad memories come up.	一些不好的回憶會出現。
But my song makes them better.	但我的歌能讓它們變好。
It pushes the bad ones out.	它會除去不好的回憶。

** ─────────────────────

finally〔'faɪn̩lɪ〕*adv.* 最後

bring〔brɪŋ〕*v.* 帶來

young〔jʌŋ〕*adj.* 年輕的；幼小的

realize〔'rɪə‚laɪz〕*v.* 了解　　lucky〔'lʌkɪ〕*adj.* 幸運的

alive〔ə'laɪv〕*adj.* 活的　　regret〔rɪ'grɛt〕*v.* 後悔

come up 出現　　***push out*** 把…推出去

It is good to have a favorite song.	有一首最喜愛的歌是很好的。
You will become stronger and happier.	你會變得更堅強且更快樂。
Listen closely and it will come.	如果你仔細聽，它就會出現。
It must have a melody.	它一定要有優美的旋律。
The rhythm is important, too.	節奏也很重要。
Most important are the words.	最重要的是歌詞。
My favorite song helps me.	我最喜愛的歌能幫助我。
I think everyone should have one.	我認為每個人都應該要有一首最喜愛的歌曲。
They always mean a lot!	它們總是意義重大！

** ————————————————————

become 〔 bɪˋkʌm 〕 *v.* 變得
closely 〔ˋkloslɪ 〕 *adv.* 仔細地　　come 〔 kʌm 〕 *v.* 出現
melody 〔ˋmɛlədɪ 〕 *n.* 旋律；優美的音樂
rhythm 〔ˋrɪðəm 〕 *n.* 節奏
important 〔 ɪmˋpɔrtn̩t 〕 *adj.* 重要的
mean 〔 min 〕 *v.* 具有意義　　*mean a lot* 意義重大

▣ 背景說明

　　音樂無國界，不論是西洋或東洋歌曲，只要是好聽的音樂，就會廣受好評。每個人心中都有一些歌曲是拿來抒發情緒或激勵自己，像是情緒低落的時候，就聽首輕快的歌來轉換心情；失戀的時候，就聽首悲傷情歌讓自己大哭特哭。因此，音樂不只是藝術，還能為我們帶來感動。

4

1. *This song brings back memories.*

   bring back 使想起　　memory〔'mɛmərɪ〕*n.* 回憶

   　　bring back 字面的意思是「帶回來」，引申為「使人想起」，所以這句話字面的意思是「這首歌將回憶帶回來。」引申為「這首歌使我想起往事。」也可說成：

   This song makes me remember many things.
   （這首歌使我想起很多事。）

   This song makes me nostalgic.
   （這首歌使我充滿懷舊的情緒。）

   This song reminds me of things.
   （這首歌使我想起一些事。）

   remember〔rɪ'mɛmbɚ〕*v.* 想起
   nostalgic〔nɑ'stældʒɪk〕*adj.* 懷舊的
   remind〔rɪ'maɪnd〕*v.* 使想起
   remind *sb.* ***of*** *sth.* 使某人想起某事

2. ***The words spoke to me.***

  words〔wɜdz〕*n. pl.* 歌詞　　***speak to*** 動（人）心弦

　　這句話字面的意思是「歌詞在對我說話。」引申為「歌詞打動我的心。」也可說成：

  The words had great meaning for me.
  （歌詞對我有很大的意義。）

  The words seemed to be directed at me.
  （歌詞似乎是針對我而寫的。）

  The words moved me.（歌詞使我感動。）

  great〔gret〕*adj.* 很大的　　meaning〔'minɪŋ〕*n.* 意義
  seem〔sim〕*v.* 似乎　　direct〔də'rɛkt〕*v.* 使針對
  be directed at 針對　　move〔muv〕*v.* 使感動

3. ***It lifted me up when I was down.***

  lift *sb.* ***up*** 使某人振作　　down〔daʊn〕*adj.* 情緒低落的

　　lift *sb.* ***up*** 的字面意思是「把某人舉起來」，在此引申為「使某人振作」。這句話的意思是「當我情緒低落時，它能使我振作。」也可說成：

  It made me feel better when I was sad.
  （當我悲傷的時候，它能使我覺得好些。）

  It cheered me up when I was depressed.
  （當我沮喪的時候，它能使我振作。）

  It made me happy when I was not.
  （當我不快樂的時候，它能使我快樂。）

  【***cheer*** *sb.* ***up*** 使某人振作　　depressed〔dɪ'prɛst〕*adj.* 沮喪的】

4. *It helps me push through difficult parts.*

　push through 設法完成

　difficult 〔'dɪfəˌkʌlt〕 *adj.* 困難的　　part〔part〕*n.* 部分

　　　　push through 字面的意思是「推過去」，奮力突破重圍，引申爲「設法完成」，所以這句話的意思是「它幫助我完成困難的部分。」也可説成：

　　It helps me keep going through the hard parts.
　　（它幫助我持續完成困難的部分。）

　　It helps me finish the difficult exercises.
　　（它有助於我完成困難的運動。）

　　It keeps me going when the exercise is tough.
　　（當運動很困難時，它能使我持續下去。）

　　keep〔kip〕*v.* 持續　　*go through* 完成
　　hard〔hard〕*adj.* 困難的　　finish〔'fɪnɪʃ〕*v.* 完成
　　keep going 持續進行　　tough〔tʌf〕*adj.* 困難的

5. *I can sing it all day long.*

　all day long 整天

　　　　這句話的意思是「我可以唱這首歌唱一整天。」也可説成：

　　I can sing it nonstop.（我可以不停地唱這首歌。）

　　I can sing it for a long time.（我可以唱這首歌唱很久。）

　　I can just keep on singing it.
　　（我可以就是一直不停地唱這首歌。）

　　【nonstop〔'nɑn'stɑp〕*adv.* 不停地　　*keep on* + *V-ing* 持續…】

6. ***But I keep going.***

keep going 持續進行

        這句話字面的意思是「但是我會持續進行。」在此引申為「但是我會持續地唱。」也可說成：

    But I don't. (但是我沒有停止。)

    But I keep singing. (但是我會持續地唱。)

    But I continue to sing. (但是我會繼續唱。)

    【continue〔kən'tɪnjʊ〕v. 繼續】

7. ***Some bad memories come up.***

come up 出現

        come up 字面的意思是「上來」，引申為「出現」，所以這句話的意思是「一些不好的回憶會出現。」也可說成：

    I remember some bad things.
    (我會想起一些不好的事。)

    I recall some bad times.
    (我會想起一些不好的時光。)

    Some bad memories appear.
    (一些不好的回憶會出現。)

    recall〔rɪ'kɔl〕v. 想起
    appear〔ə'pɪr〕v. 出現

8. *It pushes the bad ones out*.
   push out 把…推出去

   ones 在此是指 memories（回憶）。要把不好的回憶從腦海裡推出去，所以這句話引申爲「它會除去不好的回憶。」也可説成：

   > It makes me forget the bad memories.
   > （它會讓我忘記不好的回憶。）
   > It gets rid of the bad memories.
   > （它會消除不好的回憶。）
   > It takes the place of the bad memories.
   > （它會取代不好的回憶。）
   > forget〔fɚˋgɛt〕*v.* 忘記　　***get rid of*** 除去
   > ***take the place of*** 代替

9. *Listen closely and it will come*.
   closely〔ˋkloslɪ〕*adv.* 仔細地
   come〔kʌm〕*v.* 出現

   come 的基本意思是「來」，在此是作「出現」解。而「祈使句(,) and + S. + V.」則作「如果…，就～」（= *If you*…, *you*～）解，所以 Listen closely and it will come. 就等於 If you listen closely, it will come.，意思是「如果你仔細聽，它就會出現。」也可説成：

Listen carefully and you will find your song.

（如果你仔細聽，你就會找到你的歌。）

Listen closely and you will hear your song.

（如果你仔細聽，你將會聽到屬於你的歌。）

Listen carefully and your song will come to you.

（如果你仔細聽，你的歌曲就會來到你身邊。）

【carefully〔ˈkɛrfəlɪ〕*adv.* 仔細地】

　　「祈使句(,) and＋S.＋V.」這個句型作「如果…，就～」解，其用法舉例如下：

Look outside, *and* you will see my new car.

（如果你往外看，你就會看到我的新車。）

Listen closely, *and* you will hear the birds singing.

（如果你仔細聽，你就會聽到鳥在唱歌。）

Stop smoking, *and* you will feel better.

（如果你停止抽煙，你就會感覺好些。）

【outside〔ˈaʊtˈsaɪd〕*adv.* 向外面　　smoke〔smok〕*v.* 抽煙】

10. *They always mean a lot!*

mean〔min〕*v.* 具有意義　　*mean a lot* 意義重大

　　這句話的意思是「它們總是意義重大！」也可說成：

They are always meaningful!（它們總是很有意義！）

They are always important!（它們總是很重要！）

They are always special!（它們總是很特別！）

meaningful〔ˈminɪŋfəl〕*adj.* 有意義的
special〔ˈspɛʃəl〕*adj.* 特別的

 作文範例

My Favorite Song

Music plays a big part in our lives. Many people have a favorite song, and I do, too. It's a tune that I enjoy listening to, one that always makes me feel good. I first heard my song many years ago, but it still means a lot to me.

There are several reasons that I like my song. *First of all*, it is about me. The first time I heard it on the radio, its words spoke to me. It made me feel strong. Now I listen to it in the morning. It helps me think and wake up. I also listen to it before tests to give myself confidence. *Second*, it's a great song to exercise to. It helps me push through the difficult parts and finish my routine. *Third*, it's easy to remember. I can sing it any time I want and teach it to my friends. *Finally*, it brings back memories of my childhood, which was a happy time.

In short, my song makes me stronger and happier, and it inspires me to do my best. *In my opinion*, everyone should have a favorite song.

4

📖 中文翻譯

我最喜愛的歌曲

音樂在我們的生活中，扮演一個很重要的角色。許多人都有一首最喜愛的歌曲，我也有。它是一首我很喜歡聽的歌曲，總是能讓我心情很好。我第一次聽到這首歌是在很多年以前，但它對我來說仍然意義重大。

我喜歡這首歌有幾個理由。首先，它正是在說我。我第一次在廣播聽到它，它的歌詞就打動我的心。它讓我覺得我很堅強。現在，我會在早上聽這首歌。它有助於我思考並清醒。我也會在考試前聽，好讓自己有信心。第二，它是一首可以讓人運動時聽的好歌。它能幫助我完成困難的部分，完成我日常必須做的運動。第三，它很容易記。每當我想要教我的朋友時，我都可以唱出來。最後，它使我想起童年的回憶，那是一段快樂的時光。

總之，我最喜愛的歌曲讓我變得更堅強，而且更快樂，並且能激發我盡全力。我認為，每個人都應該要有一首自己最喜愛的歌。

5. My Favorite TV Show

Hi, ladies and gentlemen.
It's nice to see everyone here.
Thank you very much for listening.

Almost everyone watches television.
There are so many shows to choose from.
But in my mind, one really stands out.

It's a show that anybody can watch.
It's truly one of my favorites.
Let me tell you about Wild Kingdom.

5

favorite〔'fevərɪt〕
almost〔'ɔl,most〕
choose〔tʃuz〕
in my mind
anybody〔'ɛnɪ,badɪ〕
wild〔waɪld〕

show〔ʃo〕
television〔'tɛlə,vɪʒən〕
mind〔maɪnd〕
stand out
truly〔'trulɪ〕
kingdom〔'kɪŋdəm〕

Wild Kingdom teaches us about animals.

There are so many different kinds.

The show can teach us about each one.

We can learn how long a giraffe's neck is.

We can learn how many teeth sharks have.

We can learn how long turtles can live.

Each animal is unique.

Each one has its own special

characteristics.

Wild Kingdom lets us see them up close.

---

teach〔titʃ〕

different〔'dɪfrənt〕

learn〔lɜn〕

neck〔nɛk〕

shark〔ʃɑrk〕

live〔lɪv〕

special〔'spɛʃəl〕

characteristic〔‚kærɪktə'rɪstɪk〕

animal〔'ænəml̩〕

kind〔kaɪnd〕

giraffe〔dʒə'ræf〕

teeth〔tiθ〕

turtle〔'tɜtl̩〕

unique〔ju'nik〕

up close

We can also learn English from the show.

Wild Kingdom is in English.

But there are subtitles in case we don't
   understand.

We can improve our listening skills.

We can increase our vocabulary.

We can even improve our pronunciation.

Wild Kingdom can better our English.

If we want to, we can also take notes.

Just listening to the show can help a lot.

5

---

subtitle（'sʌb,taɪtl̩ ）	*in case*
understand（,ʌndɚ'stænd ）	improve（ ɪm'pruv ）
skill（ skɪl ）	increase（ ɪn'kris ）
vocabulary（ və'kæbjə,lɛrɪ ）	
pronunciation（ prə,nʌnsɪ'eʃən ）	
better（'bɛtɚ ）	note（ not ）
take notes	*a lot*

Wild Kingdom is fit for everyone.

It's watched by teens and adults.

Even babies can enjoy the show.

The show is very informative.

It is okay for all age levels.

It is easy to understand.

Wild Kingdom is for people of all ages.

It doesn't matter if we are 7 or 70.

I mean, who doesn't like animals?

---

fit〔fɪt〕   teens〔tinz〕

adult〔əˈdʌlt〕   baby〔ˈbebɪ〕

enjoy〔ɪnˈdʒɔɪ〕

informative〔ɪnˈfɔrmətɪv〕

okay〔ˈoˈke〕   age〔edʒ〕

level〔ˈlɛvḷ〕   easy〔ˈizɪ〕

matter〔ˈmætɚ〕   mean〔min〕

*But most of all, the show is so much fun
   to watch!*
Wild Kingdom is never boring.
Watching animals is really interesting.

Wild animals can be cute.
Wild animals can be funny.
Sometimes, wild animals can be scary.

Wild Kingdom is very exciting.
There's no telling what the animals will do.
The show keeps us on the edge of our seats.

5

---

most of all
boring ('borɪŋ)
cute (kjut)
sometimes ('sʌm,taɪmz)
exciting (ɪk'saɪtɪŋ)
tell (tɛl)
edge (ɛdʒ)
on the edge of one's seat

never ('nɛvɚ)
interesting ('ɪntrɪstɪŋ)
funny ('fʌnɪ)
scary ('skɛrɪ)
There is no V-ing
keep (kip)
seat (sit)

In short**, **Wild Kingdom is a great show.

It is my favorite TV program.

There's something in it for everyone.

We can watch almost anything on TV.

But Wild Kingdom is not only educational.

Wild Kingdom is very entertaining
  as well.

Would you like to find out about animals?

Do you like shows that are filled with fun?

Be sure to watch Wild Kingdom!

------

in short	**great** 〔 gret 〕
program 〔'progræm 〕	**something** 〔'sʌmθɪŋ 〕
anything 〔'ɛnɪˌθɪŋ 〕	**educational** 〔ˌɛdʒə'keʃənļ 〕
entertaining 〔ˌɛntɚ'tenɪŋ 〕	
as well	***find out about***
be filled with	***be sure to V.***

5. **My Favorite TV Show**

Hi, *ladies and gentlemen*.
It's nice to see everyone here.
Thank you very much for listening.

Almost everyone watches television.
There are so many shows to
　choose from.
But in my mind, one really
　stands out.

It's a show that anybody can
　watch.
It's truly one of my favorites.
Let me tell you about Wild
　Kingdom.

嗨，各位先生，各位女士。
很高興看到大家來這裡。
非常感謝你們的聆聽。

幾乎每個人都會看電視。
有很多的節目可以選擇。

但是我認為，有一個節目眞的
很出色。

它是一個任何人都可以收看的
節目。
它眞的是我最喜愛的節目之一。
讓我來告訴你們「野生王國」。

5

**

favorite〔'fevərɪt〕*adj.* 最喜愛的　*n.* 最喜愛的人或物
show〔ʃo〕*n.* 節目　　almost〔'ɔl,most〕*adv.* 幾乎
television〔'tɛlə,vɪʒən〕*n.* 電視　　choose〔tʃuz〕*v.* 選擇
mind〔maɪnd〕*n.* 心；想法　　***in my mind*** 我認為
stand out 傑出；突出　　anybody〔'ɛnɪ,bɑdɪ〕*pron.* 任何人
truly〔'trulɪ〕*adv.* 眞正地
wild〔waɪld〕*adj.* 野生的　　kingdom〔'kɪŋdəm〕*n.* 王國

Wild Kingdom teaches us about animals.

There are so many different kinds.

The show can teach us about each one.

We can learn how long a giraffe's neck is.

We can learn how many teeth sharks have.

We can learn how long turtles can live.

Each animal is unique.

Each one has its own special characteristics.

Wild Kingdom lets us see them up close.

「野生王國」使我們認識動物。

動物有許多不同的種類。

這個節目可以使我們認識每一種。

我們可以知道長頸鹿的脖子有多長。

我們可以知道鯊魚有多少顆牙齒。

我們可以知道海龜能活多久。

每個動物都很獨特。

每個動物都有牠自己的特色。

「野生王國」讓我們能近距離地看牠們。

** ————————————

teach〔titʃ〕v. 教導　　animal〔'ænəml̩〕n. 動物

different〔'dɪfrənt〕adj. 不同的　　kind〔kaɪnd〕n. 種類

learn〔lɝn〕v. 學習；得知　　giraffe〔dʒə'ræf〕n. 長頸鹿

neck〔nɛk〕n. 脖子　　teeth〔tiθ〕n. pl. 牙齒【單數是 tooth】

shark〔ʃɑrk〕n. 鯊魚　　turtle〔'tɝtl̩〕n. 海龜　　live〔lɪv〕v. 活

unique〔ju'nik〕adj. 獨特的　　special〔'spɛʃəl〕adj. 特別的

characteristic〔͵kærɪktə'rɪstɪk〕n. 特性；特色

up close 逼近地；近距離地

We can also learn English from the show.

Wild Kingdom is in English.

But there are subtitles in case we don't understand.

我們也可以從節目中學習英文。

「野生王國」是英語發音。

但是它有字幕，免得我們不了解。

We can improve our listening skills.

We can increase our vocabulary.

We can even improve our pronunciation.

我們可以增進我們的聽力。

我們可以增加字彙量。

我們甚至可以改善我們的發音。

Wild Kingdom can better our English.

If we want to, we can also take notes.

Just listening to the show can help a lot.

「野生王國」可以改善我們的英文能力。

如果我們想要的話，也可以做筆記。

只要聽這個節目，就能有很大的幫助。

5

** ————————————————————

subtitle〔'sʌb‚taɪtl̩〕*n.* 字幕　　***in case*** 以防萬一；免得
understand〔‚ʌndə'stænd〕*v.* 了解
improve〔ɪm'pruv〕*v.* 改善；增進　　skill〔skɪl〕*n.* 技能
increase〔ɪn'kris〕*v.* 增加　　vocabulary〔və'kæbjə‚lɛrɪ〕*n.* 字彙
pronunciation〔prə‚nʌnsɪ'eʃən〕*n.* 發音　　better〔'bɛtə〕*v.* 改善
note〔not〕*n.* 筆記　　***take notes*** 做筆記　　***a lot*** 大大地

Wild Kingdom is fit for everyone.	「野生王國」適合每個人觀賞。
It's watched by teens and adults.	青少年和成年人都會收看它。
Even babies can enjoy the show.	甚至連嬰兒也會喜歡這個節目。
The show is very informative.	這個節目能提供很多知識。
It is okay for all age levels.	所有年齡層都可以收看。
It is easy to understand.	內容容易了解。
Wild Kingdom is for people of all ages.	「野生王國」適合所有年齡的觀衆。
It doesn't matter if we are 7 or 70.	不論我們是七歲或七十歲，都沒關係。
I mean, who doesn't like animals?	我的意思是，誰不喜歡動物呢？

** ————————————————

fit〔fɪt〕*adj.* 適合的　　teens〔tinz〕*n. pl.* 青少年 (= *teenagers*)

adult〔ə'dʌlt〕*n.* 成人　　baby〔'bebɪ〕*n.* 嬰兒

enjoy〔ɪn'dʒɔɪ〕*v.* 享受；喜歡

informative〔ɪn'fɔrmətɪv〕*adj.* 有教育性的；提供知識的

okay〔'o'ke〕*adj.* 可以的；不錯的　　age〔edʒ〕*n.* 年齡

level〔'lɛvḷ〕*n.* 階層　　easy〔'izɪ〕*adj.* 容易的

matter〔'mætɚ〕*v.* 有關係；重要　　mean〔min〕*v.* 意思是

But most of all**, **the show is so much fun to watch!	但最重要的是，收看這個節目是很有趣的！
Wild Kingdom is never boring.	「野生王國」絕不會無聊。
Watching animals is really interesting.	觀察動物真的是很有趣。
Wild animals can be cute.	野生動物可能是可愛的。
Wild animals can be funny.	野生動物可能是逗趣的。
Sometimes, wild animals can be scary.	有時候，野生動物也可能是很可怕的。
Wild Kingdom is very exciting.	「野生王國」很令人興奮。
There's no telling what the animals will do.	我們無法知道動物將會做什麼。
The show keeps us on the edge of our seats.	這個節目會使我們一直迫不及待想知道。

**

most of all 最重要的是（= *most important of all*）
never〔ˋnɛvɚ〕*adv.* 絕不　　boring〔ˋborɪŋ〕*adj.* 無聊的
interesting〔ˋɪntrɪstɪŋ〕*adj.* 有趣的　　cute〔kjut〕*adj.* 可愛的
funny〔ˋfʌnɪ〕*adj.* 逗人發笑的；好笑的
sometimes〔ˋsʌm͵taɪmz〕*adv.* 有時候
scary〔ˋskɛrɪ〕*adj.* 可怕的；嚇人的
exciting〔ɪkˋsaɪtɪŋ〕*adj.* 令人興奮的
There is no V-ing 不可能…（= *It is impossible to V.*）
tell〔tɛl〕*v.* 知道　　keep〔kip〕*v.* 使維持（某種狀態）
edge〔ɛdʒ〕*n.* 邊緣　　seat〔sit〕*n.* 座位
on the edge of one's seat 緊張地；迫不及待（想知道）

***In short**, Wild Kingdom is a great show*.	總之，「野生王國」是一個很棒的節目。
It is my favorite TV program.	它是我最喜愛的電視節目。
There's something in it for everyone.	每個人在這個節目中都會有想看的內容。
We can watch almost anything on TV.	我們在電視上，幾乎什麼都看得到。
But Wild Kingdom is not only educational.	但「野生王國」不僅有教育意義。
Wild Kingdom is very entertaining as well.	「野生王國」也非常有趣。
Would you like to find out about animals?	你想查明有關動物的資料嗎？
Do you like shows that are filled with fun?	你喜歡充滿樂趣的節目嗎？
Be sure to watch Wild Kingdom!	一定要收看「野生王國」！

** ─────────────────────

in short 簡言之；總之　　**great** 〔 gret 〕 *adj.* 很棒的
program 〔 ˋprogræm 〕 *n.* 節目
something 〔 ˋsʌmθɪŋ 〕 *pron.* 某事；某物
anything 〔 ˋɛnɪ͵θɪŋ 〕 *pron.* 任何東西；什麼都
educational 〔 ͵ɛdʒəˋkeʃənl̩ 〕 *adj.* 有教育意義的
entertaining 〔 ͵ɛntɚˋtenɪŋ 〕 *adj.* 令人愉快的；有趣的
as well 也（= *too*）　　***find out about*** 查明關於…的事實
be filled with 充滿了　　***be sure to V.*** 一定要…

📖 背景說明

　　看電視是現代人的娛樂之一。電視節目的類型
多，有電影類、綜藝類、音樂類、知性類等，有那
麼多種類可供選擇，難怪很多人假日就變成 couch
potato（整天坐在沙發上看電視的人）。本篇演講稿
要介紹一個有趣的電視節目。

1. ***But in my mind, one really stands out.***

mind〔maɪnd〕*n.* 心；想法　　***in my mind*** 我認為
stand out 傑出；突出

　　in my mind 字面的意思是「在我的想法中」，引申
為「我認為」。***stand out*** 字面的意思是「站出來」，就像是
鶴立雞群一樣，所以引申為「傑出；突出」。這句話的意
思是「但是我認為，有一個節目真的很出色。」也可說成：

In my opinion, one is the best.
（依我看來，有一個節目是最棒的。）

To my mind, one is special.
（我認為，有一個節目是很特別的。）

But I think there is one that is different from
all the rest.
（但是我認為，有一個節目和所有其他的節目不一樣。）

in one's opinion 依某人之見
to one's mind 依某人的想法
special〔'spɛʃəl〕*adj.* 特別的
different〔'dɪfrənt〕*adj.* 不同的　　rest〔rɛst〕*n.* 其餘之物

5

2. *Wild Kingdom lets us see them up close.*

wild〔waɪld〕*adj.* 野生的   kingdom〔'kɪŋdəm〕*n.* 王國
up close 近在咫尺；接近

　　　這句話的意思是「『野生王國』讓我們能近距離地看牠們。」也可說成：

Wild Kingdom allows us to get a good look at
　them. (「野生王國」使我們能仔細地看牠們。)

Wild Kingdom lets us get close to them.
(「野生王國」讓我們能接近牠們。)

Wild Kingdom brings us close to them.
(「野生王國」使我們接近牠們。)

allow〔ə'laʊ〕*v.* 使能夠   *have a good look at* 仔細地看
close〔klos〕*adj.* 接近的

3. *Wild Kingdom is in English.*

　　　這句話的意思是「『野生王國』是英語發音。」也可說成：

Wild Kingdom is an English program.
(「野生王國」是英語節目。)

It's broadcast in English.
(「野生王國」是用英語播出。)

The people on the show speak English.
(節目裡的人是說英語的。)

program〔'prog ræm〕*n.* 節目
broadcast〔'brɔd‚kæst〕*v.* 播送

4. *But there are subtitles in case we don't understand.*

subtitle〔'sʌb‚taɪtl̩〕*n.* 字幕

in case 以防萬一；免得

understand〔‚ʌndɚ'stænd〕*v.* 了解

　　這句話的意思是「但是它有字幕，免得我們不了解。」也可説成：

But we can read the subtitles if we don't
　understand.
（但是如果我們不了解，我們可以看字幕。）

But there are also Chinese subtitles.
（但是也有中文字幕。）

If we can't understand the English,
　we can read the subtitles.
（如果我們不懂英文，我們可以看字幕。）

【Chinese〔tʃaɪ'niz〕*adj.* 中文的】

5

　　case 的意思是「情況」，*in case* 表示爲了可能發生的情況作準備，因而引申爲「以防萬一；免得」，其用法舉例如下：

I'll bring an umbrella *in case* it rains.
（我會帶雨傘以防下雨。）

Please give me your phone number *in case*
　I get lost.
（請給我你的電話號碼，以防我會迷路。）

We keep a flashlight in the drawer *in case* the
　　electricity is cut off.

（我們在抽屜放了手電筒，以防停止供電。）

umbrella〔ʌmˋbrɛlə〕*n.* 雨傘
rain〔ren〕*v.* 下雨
phone〔fon〕*n.* 電話
number〔ˋnʌmbɚ〕*n.* 號碼
get lost 迷路　　　flashlight〔ˋflæʃˏlaɪt〕*n.* 手電筒
drawer〔drɔr〕*n.* 抽屜
electricity〔ɪˏlɛkˋtrɪsətɪ〕*n.* 電　　***cut off*** 切斷

5. *Wild Kingdom can better our English.*

better〔ˋbɛtɚ〕*v.* 改善

　　　better 主要是當形容詞用，作「更好的」解，在此
是當動詞用，作「改善」解。這句話的意思是「『野生
王國』可以改善我們的英文能力。」也可說成：

It can improve our English.

（它可以增進我們的英文能力。）

It can help us advance in English.

（它可以幫助我們在英文上有進步。）

It can help us develop our English.

（它可以幫助我們培養英文能力。）

improve〔ɪmˋpruv〕*v.* 改善；使進步
advance〔ədˋvæns〕*v.* 進步
develop〔dɪˋvɛləp〕*v.* 培養

6. *But most of all, the show is so much fun to watch!*

most of all 最重要的是（= *most important of all* ）
show〔ʃo〕*n.* 節目

這句話的意思是「但最重要的是，收看這個節目是很有趣的！」也可說成：

But most of all, Wild Kingdom is great fun to watch!
（但最重要的是，收看「野生王國」是很有趣的！）

But most important of all, the program is very entertaining!
（但最重要的是，這個節目很有趣！）

But best of all, we can have a lot of fun watching the show!
（但最好的一點是，我們看這個節目會很開心！）

program〔'progræm〕*n.* 節目
entertaining〔ˌɛntɚ'tenɪŋ〕*adj.* 有趣的
best of all 最好的一點是　　*have fun* 玩得開心

5

7. *There's no telling what the animals will do.*

There is no V-ing 不可能⋯（= *It is impossible to V.* ）
tell〔tɛl〕*v.* 知道

tell 的基本意思是「說」，在此是作「知道」解。這句話的意思是「我們無法知道動物將會做什麼。」也可說成：

No one can predict what the animals
   will do.

（沒人能預測到動物將會做什麼。）

The animals could do anything.

（動物可能會做任何事。）

We can't be sure how the animals
   will behave.

（我們無法確定動物將會有怎樣的行爲。）

predict〔 prɪˋdɪkt 〕 *v.* 預測
anything〔ˋɛnɪˏθɪŋ 〕 *pron.* 任何事物；什麼都
sure〔 ʃʊr 〕 *adj.* 確定的
behave〔 bɪˋhev 〕 *v.* 行爲；表現

8. *The show keeps us on the edge of our seats.*

keep〔 kip 〕 *v.* 使維持（某種狀態）

edge〔 ɛdʒ 〕 *n.* 邊緣   seat〔 sit 〕 *n.* 座位

on the edge of one's seat 緊張地；迫不及待（想知道）

　　　on the edge of one's seat 字面的意思是「在某人座位的邊緣」，當一個人很想知道接下來即將發生的事，而感到興奮或緊張時，會越坐越前面，所以引申爲「緊張地；迫不及待（想知道）」。這句話的意思是「這個節目會使我們一直迫不及待想知道。」也可說成：

The show keeps us in suspense.

（這個節目使我們感到懸疑緊張。）

The show keeps us interested.

（這個節目使我們很有興趣。）

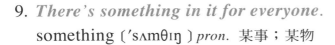

The show keeps us enthralled.

（這個節目使我們著迷。）

suspense〔sə'spɛns〕*n.* 懸疑；持續的緊張
keep** sb. **in suspense 使某人懸疑緊張
interested〔'ɪntrɪstɪd〕*adj.* 有興趣的
enthralled〔ɪn'θrɔld〕*adj.* 著迷的

9. ***There's something in it for everyone.***

something〔'sʌmθɪŋ〕*pron.* 某事；某物

這句話字面的意思是「它裡面有某些東西要給每個人。」引申為「每個人在這個節目中都會有想看的內容。」也可說成：

Everyone can find something interesting in the show.

（每個人在這個節目中，都可以找到有趣的內容。）

Something in the show will appeal to everyone.

（這個節目的某些內容會吸引每個人。）

Everyone can find something in the show that he likes.

（每個人都會在這個節目中，找到自己喜歡的某些內容。）

find〔faɪnd〕*v.* 找到　interesting〔'ɪntrɪstɪŋ〕*adj.* 有趣的
appeal〔ə'pil〕*v.* 有吸引力　***appeal to*** 吸引

10. *Would you like to find out about animals?*

find out about 查明關於…的事實

這句話的意思是「你想查明有關動物的資料嗎？」
也可說成：

Would you like to know more about animals?
（你想知道更多關於動物的事嗎？）

Do you want more information about animals?
（你想知道更多關於動物的資料嗎？）

Are you curious about animals?
（你對動物好奇嗎？）

information〔͵ɪnfəˋmeʃən〕*n.* 資訊；資料
curious〔ˋkjʊrɪəs〕*adj.* 好奇的；想知道的

11. *Be sure to watch Wild Kingdom!*

be sure to V. 一定要…

這句話的意思是「一定要收看『野生王國』！」
也可說成：

Then you should watch Wild Kingdom!
（那麼你應該要收看「野生王國」！）

Tune in to Wild Kingdom!
（收看「野生王國」吧！）

Don't miss Wild Kingdom!
（不要錯過「野生王國」！）

then〔ðɛn〕*adv.* 那麼　　***tune in to***　（調整頻道）收看
miss〔mɪs〕*v.* 錯過

 作文範例

My Favorite TV Show

Television is one of the most popular entertainments today. There is a wide variety of programs to choose from. Some are entertaining; some are educational. My favorite show is a little of both. Its name is Wild Kingdom.

Wild Kingdom is my favorite TV program because it can teach me a lot while being fun to watch. The show is about animals, so of course I can learn about animals and their behavior. Wild Kingdom lets me see them up close, which is amazing, and much more fun than reading about them in a book. *In addition*, the content is easy to understand, so it is a suitable show for people of all ages. The program can also teach me English, because it is filmed in English. Just by watching the show I can improve my vocabulary and listening skills. *Finally*, the show is never boring. There's no telling what wild animals will do, and the suspense keeps me on the edge of my seat.

In short, Wild Kingdom is a great TV show. It is not only entertaining, but also educational. Watching this wonderful program is a fun way to learn something new.

5

📖 中文翻譯

我最喜愛的電視節目

　　電視是現在最受歡迎的娛樂之一。有很多各式各樣的節目可以選擇。有些是娛樂性的；有些是教育性的。我最喜愛的節目則是兩者的性質都有一點。它的名稱是「野生王國」。

　　「野生王國」是我最喜愛的電視節目，因為收看它很有趣，同時也可以教我很多事情。這個節目是關於動物的，因此我當然也可以得知與動物有關的資訊和牠們的行為。「野生王國」讓我能近距離地看牠們，這跟在書上看到的比起來，更令人驚奇，而且更有趣。此外，它的內容相當淺顯易懂，所以它是一個適合各個年齡的民眾收看的節目。這個節目也可以教我英文，因為它是用英語拍攝的。只要藉由收看這個節目，我就可以增進我的字彙量和聽力。最後，這個節目絕不會無聊。我們無法知道野生動物會做些什麼，而那種懸疑緊張感使我迫不及待想知道。

　　總之，「野生王國」是一個很棒的電視節目。它不僅有娛樂性，也有教育性。收看這個精彩的節目，是一個能學習新事物的有趣方式。

6. The Internet and I

Please make yourselves comfortable.
It's nice that we could meet today.
Please sit back and enjoy the speech.

The best mass media is the Internet.
It can provide so many services!
People use it to stay together.

The Internet has many uses.
I would like to share a few with you.
Here goes!

6

Internet〔'ɪntɚˌnɛt 〕   *Make yourself comfortable.*
meet〔 mit 〕   *sit back*
media〔'midɪə 〕   *mass media*
provide〔 prə'vaɪd 〕   service〔'sɝvɪs 〕
use〔 juz 〕   stay〔 ste 〕
stay together   use〔 jus 〕
share〔 ʃɛr 〕   *a few*
Here goes!

First, *the Internet gives information.*
I can visit interesting websites.
There is information on many things.

I can learn about physics.
I can watch videos on history.
I can find weather information.

I can learn about waves at
   many beaches.
I can watch surfers ride the waves.
With the Internet I can see it all.

---

first〔f3st〕   give〔gɪv〕

information〔ˌɪnfə'meʃən〕   visit〔'vɪzɪt〕

interesting〔'ɪntrɪstɪŋ〕   website〔'wɛbˌsaɪt〕

learn about   physics〔'fɪzɪks〕

video〔'vɪdɪˌo〕   on〔ɑn〕

history〔'hɪstrɪ〕   find〔faɪnd〕

weather〔'wɛðə〕   wave〔wev〕

beach〔bitʃ〕   surfer〔'sɜfə〕

ride〔raɪd〕   *ride the waves*

Also, *I can stay in touch*.

E-mail and chat rooms are excellent.

It is just like being with my friends!

I am able to share stories.

I can hear about current events.

News from around the world is here.

Blogs bring ideas from many people.

I can log on and post my thoughts.

My blog gives me my own space
   on the Net.

6

---

stay in touch	e-mail (ˈiˌmel)
chat room	excellent (ˈɛkslə̣nt)
like (laɪk)	*be able to V*.
current (ˈkɝənt)	event (ɪˈvɛnt)
current events	news (njuz)
around the world	blog (blɑg)
idea (aɪˈdiə)	*log on*
post (post)	thought (θɔt)
own (on)	space (spes)
the Net	

***Third*, *many games are available*.**

Some I can download.

Some I can play with others online.

The best games are colorful and real.

They are exciting.

They let me enter another world.

Many games are changeable.

They keep up with our lives!

Spending time with them is fun.

---

third〔θ₃d〕

available〔ə'veləbḷ〕

online〔'ɑn,laɪn〕

real〔'riəl〕

enter〔'ɛntɚ〕

keep up with

spend〔spɛnd〕

game〔gem〕

download〔'daʊn,lod〕

colorful〔'kʌləfəl〕

exciting〔ɪk'saɪtɪŋ〕

changeable〔'tʃendʒəbḷ〕

lives〔laɪvz〕

fun〔fʌn〕

Finally, it can help me save time
  and money.
I can read stories on the Internet.
There is no need to go to the library.

There are also many good deals
  on the Internet.
Downloading music is cheaper.
Full albums cost less on the Internet.

I can read articles on the Internet, too.
There is no cost for many of them.
They are all cheaper than magazines.

6

---

finally ('faɪnlɪ)   save (sev)
library ('laɪ,brɛrɪ)   deal (dil)
a good deal   cheap (tʃip)
full (fʊl)   album ('ælbəm)
cost (kɔst)   less (lɛs)
article ('ɑrtɪkl̩)   magazine (,mægə'zin)

The Internet is an excellent tool.

But it requires some training.

Its many functions are powerful.

I use it for everything from music
   to e-mail.

It's better than shopping at a mall!

Anyone can see its value.

The Internet is a wonderful thing.

We can do so much with it.

I can no longer imagine the world
   without it.

tool〔 tul 〕

training〔'trenɪŋ 〕

powerful〔'pauə-fəl 〕

mall〔 mɔl 〕

wonderful〔'wʌndə-fəl 〕

imagine〔 ɪ'mædʒɪn 〕

require〔 rɪ'kwaɪr 〕

function〔'fʌŋkʃən 〕

shop〔 ʃɑp 〕

value〔'vælju 〕

no longer

6. **The Internet and I**

- -

Please make yourselves comfortable.	請不要拘束。
It's nice that we could meet today.	很高興今天我們能見面。
Please sit back and enjoy the *speech*.	請靠椅背而坐，好好聽這場演說。
The best mass media is the Internet.	最好的大眾傳播媒體就是網路。
It can provide so many services!	它可以提供很多服務！
People use it to stay together.	人們利用它保持接觸。
The Internet has many uses.	網路有很多用途。
I would like to share a few with you.	我想與你們分享一些。
Here goes!	我這就開始了！

6

** ────────────────────────

Internet〔ˈɪntɚˌnɛt〕*n.* 網際網路
Make yourself comfortable. 請不要拘束。
sit back （靠椅背而）坐；舒服地坐著
media〔ˈmidɪə〕*n. pl.* 媒體　　***mass media*** 大眾傳播媒體
provide〔prəˈvaɪd〕*v.* 提供　　service〔ˈsɝvɪs〕*n.* 服務
use〔juz〕*v.* 使用；利用　〔jus〕*n.* 用途　　stay〔ste〕*v.* 保持
stay together 繼續在一起　　share〔ʃɛr〕*v.* 分享
a few 一些；幾個　　***Here goes!*** 我這就開始了！

First, *the Internet gives information*.	首先，網路能提供資訊。
I can visit interesting websites.	我可以去看有趣的網站。
There is information on many things.	有關於很多事物的資訊。
I can learn about physics.	我可以學習有關物理學的知識。
I can watch videos on history.	我可以看歷史影片。
I can find weather information.	我可以找到天氣的資訊。
I can learn about waves at many beaches.	我可以得知許多海灘的海浪狀況。
I can watch surfers ride the waves.	我可以看衝浪者衝浪。
With the Internet I can see it all.	有了網路，我全都看得到。

＊＊ ─────────────────

first〔fɝst〕*adv.* 首先　　give〔gɪv〕*v.* 提供
information〔ˌɪnfɚˋmeʃən〕*n.* 資訊　　visit〔ˋvɪzɪt〕*v.* 參觀
interesting〔ˋɪntrɪstɪŋ〕*adj.* 有趣的
website〔ˋwɛbˏsaɪt〕*n.* 網站　　***learn about*** 學習有關…的知識
physics〔ˋfɪzɪks〕*n.* 物理學　　video〔ˋvɪdɪˏo〕*n.* 錄影（節目）
on〔ɑn〕*prep.* 關於（= *about*）　　history〔ˋhɪstrɪ〕*n.* 歷史
weather〔ˋwɛðɚ〕*n.* 天氣　　wave〔wev〕*n.* 波浪
beach〔bitʃ〕*n.* 海灘　　surfer〔ˋsɝfɚ〕*n.* 衝浪者
ride〔raɪd〕*v.* 乘（風、浪等）；在…上航行前進
ride the waves 破浪前進；衝浪

Also, I can stay in touch. | 而且，我可以和大家保持連絡。

E-mail and chat rooms are excellent. | 電子郵件和聊天室都很棒。

It is just like being with my friends! | 就像和我的朋友在一起一樣！

I am able to share stories. | 我能夠分享故事。

I can hear about current events. | 我可以聽到時事。

News from around the world is here. | 世界各地的新聞都在這裡。

Blogs bring ideas from many people. | 部落格能提供許多人的想法。

I can log on and post my thoughts. | 我可以登入然後發表自己的想法。

My blog gives me my own space on the Net. | 我的部落格讓我在網路上擁有自己的空間。

**

stay in touch 保持連絡　　e-mail〔ˈiˌmel〕n. 電子郵件
chat room 聊天室　　excellent〔ˈɛkslʂnt〕adj. 極好的
like〔laɪk〕prep. 像　　be able to V. 能夠…
current〔ˈkɝ ənt〕adj. 目前的　　event〔ɪˈvɛnt〕n. 事件
current events 時事　　news〔njuz〕n. 新聞
around the world 全世界　　blog〔blɑg〕n. 部落格
idea〔aɪˈdiə〕n. 想法　　log on 登入　　post〔post〕v. 發表；貼上
thought〔θɔt〕n. 想法　　own〔on〕adj. 自己的
space〔spes〕n. 空間　　the Net 網際網路 (= the Internet)

Third, many games are available.	第三，可取得許多遊戲。
Some I can download.	有些我可以下載。
Some I can play with others online.	有些我可以在線上和其他人一起玩。
The best games are colorful and real.	最好的遊戲要生動逼真。
They are exciting.	它們很刺激。
They let me enter another world.	它們讓我進入另一個世界。
Many games are changeable.	許多遊戲常會改變。
They keep up with our lives!	它們跟得上我們的生活！
Spending time with them is fun.	花時間玩這些遊戲很有趣。

** ———————————————————

third〔θɝd〕*adv.* 第三   game〔gem〕*n.* 遊戲
available〔ə'veləbḷ〕*adj.* 可獲得的
download〔'daʊn,lod〕*v.* 下載
online〔'ɑn,laɪn〕*adv.* 在線上
colorful〔'kʌləfəl〕*adj.* 多彩多姿的；生動的
real〔'riəl〕*adj.* 真的；逼真的
exciting〔ɪk'saɪtɪŋ〕*adj.* 刺激的   enter〔'ɛntə〕*v.* 進入
changeable〔'tʃendʒəbḷ〕*adj.* 易變的；善變的
keep up with 跟上   lives〔laɪvz〕*n. pl.* 生活【單數是 life】
spend〔spɛnd〕*v.* 花費   fun〔fʌn〕*adj.* 有趣的

***Finally**, it can help me save time and money*.	最後，網路可以幫我節省時間和金錢。
I can read stories on the Internet.	我可以在網路上看小說。
There is no need to go to the library.	不必去圖書館。
There are also many good deals on the Internet.	網路上也有許多便宜的東西。
Downloading music is cheaper.	下載音樂比較便宜。
Full albums cost less on the Internet.	網路上整張專輯售價較低。
I can read articles on the Internet, too.	我也可以在網路上閱讀文章。
There is no cost for many of them.	很多都是不用錢的。
They are all cheaper than magazines.	它們都比雜誌便宜。

** ————————————————————

finally〔ˈfaɪnḷɪ〕*adv.* 最後　　save〔sev〕*v.* 節省

library〔ˈlaɪˏbrɛrɪ〕*n.* 圖書館　　deal〔dil〕*n.* 交易

a good deal 便宜貨　　cheap〔tʃip〕*adj.* 便宜的

full〔fʊl〕*adj.* 完整的　　album〔ˈælbəm〕*n.* 唱片；專輯

cost〔kɔst〕*v.* 花費　*n.* 費用　　less〔lɛs〕*adv.* 較少

article〔ˈɑrtɪkḷ〕*n.* 文章　　magazine〔ˏmægəˈzin〕*n.* 雜誌

The Internet is an excellent tool.   網路是很好的工具。

But it requires some training.   但是它需要一些訓練。

Its many functions are powerful.   它的許多功能都很強大。

I use it for everything from   我利用它來做每件事，從
    music to e-mail.   音樂到電子郵件。

It's better than shopping at a mall!   這比去購物中心購物好！

Anyone can see its value.   任何人都能了解它的價值。

The Internet is a wonderful thing.   網路是很棒的。

We can do so much with it.   我們能用它做很多事。

I can no longer imagine the   我已經無法想像沒有它的
    world without it.   世界。

**

tool〔tul〕*n.* 工具　　require〔rɪˈkwaɪr〕*v.* 需要

training〔ˈtrenɪŋ〕*n.* 訓練；練習

function〔ˈfʌŋkʃən〕*n.* 功能

powerful〔ˈpaʊɚfəl〕*adj.* 強有力的　　shop〔ʃɑp〕*v.* 購物

mall〔mɔl〕*n.* 購物中心　　value〔ˈvælju〕*n.* 價值

wonderful〔ˈwʌndɚfəl〕*adj.* 極好的；很棒的

no longer 不再

imagine〔ɪˈmædʒɪn〕*v.* 想像

背景說明

　　隨著網路的發達，現在的人不用出門，就可以在家裡辦妥一切事情。利用線上購物，就能買衣服、鞋子，甚至是食物；利用搜尋功能，就能找到所需的資訊；利用網路銀行，就可轉帳。如果懂得好好利用網路，它的價值絕對會超乎你的想像。

1. ***People use it to stay together.***

   use〔juz〕*v.* 使用；利用　　　stay〔ste〕*v.* 保持
   stay together 繼續在一起

   　　這句話字面的意思是「人們利用它繼續在一起。」引申為「人們利用它保持接觸。」也可說成：

   > People use it to keep in touch.
   > （人們利用它保持連絡。）
   >
   > People use it to stay connected.
   > （人們利用它保持連絡。）
   >
   > People use it to stay close.
   > （人們利用它保持密切的關係。）

   keep in touch 保持連絡
   connected〔kə'nɛktɪd〕*adj.* 有連絡的
   close〔klos〕*adj.* 密切的

6

2. ***Here goes!***

go〔go〕*v.* 去；開始【源自起跑的口令】

這句話來自：Here it goes!（就要開始了！）也有
人說：Here we go!（我們就要開始了！）或 Here I go!
（我就要開始了！）美國人也常說：Let's begin!（我們
開始吧！）或 Now I'll start!（現在我就要開始了！）

3. ***I can learn about waves at many beaches.***

learn about 得知關於…的知識
wave〔wev〕*n.* 波浪
beach〔bitʃ〕*n.* 海灘

這句話的意思是「我可以得知
許多海灘的海浪狀況。」也可說成：

> I can find out about the surf conditions
> at different beaches.
> （我可以查出不同海灘的海浪狀況。）

find out about 查出關於…的資訊
surf〔sɝf〕*n.* 海浪
condition〔kənˈdɪʃən〕*n.* 狀況
different〔ˈdɪfrənt〕*adj.* 不同的

4. ***With the Internet I can see it all.***

這句話的意思是「有了網路，我全都看得到。」
也可說成：

When I use the Internet, I can see everything.
（當我使用網路的時候，我可以看見一切。）

By using the Internet, I can see whatever I want.
（藉由使用網路，無論我想看什麼都可以看到。）

With the Internet I can see anything in the world.
（有了網路，我可以看到世界上的任何東西。）

everything〔ˈɛvrɪˌθɪŋ〕*pron.* 一切事物
whatever〔hwɑtˈɛvɚ〕*pron.* 無論什麼
anything〔ˈɛnɪˌθɪŋ〕*pron.* 任何東西

5. *Also, I can stay in touch.*

also〔ˈɔlso〕*adv.* 另外　　*stay in touch* 保持連絡

　　　　這句話的意思是「而且，我可以和大家保持連絡。」
也可說成：

6

In addition, I can keep up with what is going
on in the world.
（此外，我可以隨時知道世界上發生了什麼事。）

Besides, I can connect with other people.
（此外，我可以和其他人連繫。）

Furthermore, I can be part of a community.
（此外，我可以成爲社會的一份子。）

in addition 另外　　*keep up with* 跟上
go on 發生　　besides〔bɪˈsaɪdz〕*adv.* 此外
connect〔kəˈnɛkt〕*v.* 連繫
furthermore〔ˈfɝðɚˌmor〕*adv.* 此外
community〔kəˈmjunətɪ〕*n.* 社會

6. ***They keep up with our lives!***

  keep up with 跟上   lives〔laɪvz〕*n. pl.* 生活

     這句話的意思是「它們跟得上我們的生活！」

  也可說成：

    They adapt to our lives!
    （它們會適應我們的生活！）

    They use what is going on in our lives!
    （它們會利用我們生活中發生的事！）

    They are relevant to our lives!
    （它們和我們的生活有關連！）

    adapt〔ə'dæpt〕*v.* 適應 < *to* >
    relevant〔'rɛləvənt〕*adj.* 有關連的

7. ***There are also many good deals on the Internet.***

  deal〔dil〕*n.* 交易   ***a good deal*** 便宜貨

     deal 的意思是「交易」，而 ***a good deal*** 字面的意思
  是「好的交易」，引申為「便宜貨」，其用法舉例如下：

    That car was ***a good deal***. We saved $2,000.
    （那輛車很便宜。我們省了兩千美元。）

    The daily special at the restaurant is ***a good deal***.
    （這間餐廳的每日特餐都很划算。）

    save〔sev〕*v.* 節省   daily〔'delɪ〕*adj.* 每日的
    special〔'spɛʃəl〕*n.* 特色菜；特餐
    restaurant〔'rɛstərənt〕*n.* 餐廳

這句話的意思是「網路上也有許多便宜的東西。」
也可説成：

> There are also many good bargains on the
> Internet.（網路上也有許多便宜的東西。）

> Things are sold at a good price on the
> Internet.（網路上賣的東西價格很便宜。）

> In addition, I can buy things at a low price.
> （另外，我可以用低價買到東西。）

bargain〔ˈbɑrgɪn〕*n.* 便宜貨
price〔praɪs〕*n.* 價格　　low〔lo〕*adj.* 低的

8. ***Full albums cost less on the Internet.***
full〔fʊl〕*adj.* 完整的　　album〔ˈælbəm〕*n.* 專輯；唱片
cost〔kɔst〕*v.* 花費　　less〔lɛs〕*adv.* 較少

這句話的意思是「網路上整張專輯售價較低。」也可説成：

> It's less expensive to buy complete albums
> on the Internet.
> （在網路上買完整的專輯比較便宜。）

> It's cheaper to buy albums on the Internet.
> （在網路上買專輯比較便宜。）

> Full albums are a better buy on the Internet.
> （網路上完整的專輯比較便宜。）

expensive〔ɪkˈspɛnsɪv〕*adj.* 昂貴的
complete〔kəmˈplit〕*adj.* 完整的
buy〔baɪ〕*n.* 購買之物　　***a better buy*** 買得較便宜的東西

6

9. *I can no longer imagine the world without it.*

no longer 不再

imagine〔ɪˋmædʒɪn〕*v.* 想像

　　no longer 字面的意思是「沒有更久」，引申為「不再」。這句話的意思是「我已經無法想像沒有它的世界。」也可說成：

The world would be completely different without the Internet.
（如果沒有網路，這個世界會完全不一樣。）

I cannot imagine what the world would be like without the Internet.
（我無法想像，如果世界上沒有網路，會是什麼樣子。）

I forgot what the world was like before the Internet.
（我忘了網路出現前的世界是什麼樣子。）

completely〔kəmˋplitlɪ〕*adv.* 完全地
like〔laɪk〕*prep.* 像
forget〔fɚˋgɛt〕*v.* 忘記

 作文範例

The Internet and I

In today's world there are many ways to get information. We can read newspapers, watch television, or listen to the radio. We can also log on to the Internet. *In my opinion*, this is the most useful form of mass media.

I use the Internet to do many things. *Most importantly*, I get information from it. I can find out about physics or history, or even watch surfers ride the waves at my favorite beach. With the Internet I can see it all. *In addition*, I can stay in touch with my friends and make new acquaintances, too. I can use e-mail and visit chat rooms to keep up with what is going on. *Moreover*, I can play games with my friends online. This is a fun way to spend time. *Finally*, I can save both time and money by using the Internet. When I read articles online, I don't have to waste time going to the library or use my money to buy magazines or newspapers. I can also order many kinds of goods, and they are often cheaper than those sold in stores.

In sum, the Internet is an excellent tool. Its many functions are powerful and its value is obvious. We should all learn how to take full advantage of it.

6

📖 中文翻譯

網路與我

現在世界上有很多獲得資訊的方式。我們可以看報紙、電視，或是聽廣播。我們也可以上網。我認為，這是最有用的一種大眾傳播媒體。

我用網路做很多事。最重要的是，我能從那裡得到資訊。我可以找到關於物理或歷史的資訊，或甚至是看衝浪者在我最喜愛的海邊衝浪。有了網路，我全都看得到。此外，我也可以和朋友保持連繫，以及結識新朋友。我可以利用電子郵件和去聊天室，得知發生了什麼事。而且，我可以在線上和朋友玩遊戲。這是個有趣的打發時間的方法。最後，我可以利用網路節省時間和金錢。當我在線上閱讀文章時，我不必浪費時間到圖書館，或用我的錢買雜誌或報紙。我也可以訂購很多種商品，而且它們通常會比在商店裡賣的商品還便宜。

總之，網路是很棒的工具。它的許多功能都很強大，而且它的價值顯而易見。我們全都應該學習如何充分利用它。

7. Stress in Teenagers

Good evening, ladies and gentlemen.
Thank you for being here.
It's nice to see you.

Teenagers today are very busy.
There are many things that we have to do.
It's not easy being a teenager.

My speech today is about stress.
It's something that affects every teen.
Stress in teenagers is a very real problem.

7

---

stress〔strɛs〕

teenager〔'tin,edʒɚ〕

today〔tə'de〕

busy〔'bɪzɪ〕

easy〔'izɪ〕

affect〔ə'fɛkt〕

teen〔tin〕

real〔'riəl〕

problem〔'prɑbləm〕

a real problem

First, what is stress?

It is worry or strain caused by something
   new or difficult.
We can get stress from many things.

We can feel stressed before a test.
We can feel stressed seeing a doctor.
We can even feel stressed giving a speech!

Teens have a lot of schoolwork to do.
Teens have many exams to prepare for.
Teens today are especially stressed.

---

worry〔'wɝɪ〕

cause〔kɔz〕

difficult〔'dɪfə͵kʌlt〕

test〔tɛst〕

see a doctor

schoolwork〔'skul͵wɝk〕

prepare〔prɪ'pɛr〕

strain〔stren〕

new〔nju〕

stressed〔strɛst〕

doctor〔'dɑktɚ〕

give a speech

exam〔ɪg'zæm〕

especially〔ə'spɛʃəlɪ〕

***So**, what can stress do to teenagers?*

The effects of stress are many.

Every teenager handles stress
  differently.

Some teens cry a lot.

Some teens feel bad about themselves.

Others can even get angry.

Stress is powerful.

Stress can affect our emotions.

It makes teenagers feel depressed.

7

effect〔ɪ'fɛkt〕   handle〔'hændl̩〕

differently〔'dɪfərəntlɪ〕   cry〔kraɪ〕

a lot   bad〔bæd〕

others〔'ʌðəz〕   angry〔'æŋgrɪ〕

powerful〔'paʊəfəl〕   emotion〔ɪ'moʃən〕

depressed〔dɪ'prɛst〕

Stress can also affect our bodies.

Many effects can be either seen or felt.

Here are some danger signs.

Our palms may start to sweat.

We could feel butterflies in our stomachs.

Our hearts may start beating faster.

Some teens may start to have headaches.

Others may even break out in rashes.

Teens have to be aware of these

    symptoms.

---

body〔ˈbɑdɪ〕	**either…or~**
danger〔ˈdendʒɚ〕	sign〔saɪn〕
palm〔pɑm〕	start〔stɑrt〕
sweat〔swɛt〕	butterflies〔ˈbʌtɚˌflaɪz〕
stomach〔ˈstʌmək〕	**butterflies in one's stomach**
beat〔bit〕	fast〔fæst〕
headache〔ˈhɛdˌek〕	**break out**
rash〔ræʃ〕	aware〔əˈwɛr〕
be aware of	symptom〔ˈsɪmptəm〕

So**, **what can teenagers do about stress?
There are many things we can do.
Here are some tips.

We can train ourselves to relax.
We can try to get enough sleep every night.
We can talk to people that we trust.

Most of all, we can try not to get upset
　over things we can't change.
Sometimes bad things happen to us.
We just have to grin and bear it.

7

tip〔 tɪp 〕
ourselves〔 aʊrˈsɛlvz 〕
try〔 traɪ 〕
enough〔 ɪˈnʌf , əˈnʌf 〕
trust〔 trʌst 〕
upset〔 ʌpˈsɛt 〕
happen〔ˈhæpən 〕
bear〔 bɛr 〕

train〔 tren 〕
relax〔 rɪˈlæks 〕

most of all
change〔 tʃendʒ 〕
grin〔 grɪn 〕
grin and bear it

Stress is everywhere.

It is a part of our everyday lives.

We can't escape it.

But stress isn't always a bad thing.

Without stress, we would get lazy.

Without stress, nothing would get done.

Teenagers shouldn't try to avoid stress.

We should just try to manage it better.

Take a deep breath and relax!

---

everywhere (ˈɛvrɪ͵hwɛr)   part (part)

everyday (ˈɛvrɪˈde)   escape (əˈskep)

not always   without (wɪðˈaʊt)

lazy (ˈlezɪ)   done (dʌn)

avoid (əˈvɔɪd)   manage (ˈmænɪdʒ)

better (ˈbɛtɚ)   deep (dip)

breath (brɛθ)   *take a deep breath*

7. **Stress in Teenagers**

🔊 演講解說

Good evening, ladies and gentlemen.	晚安，各位先生，各位女士。
Thank you for being here.	感謝你們的到來。
It's nice to see you.	很高興能看見你們。
Teenagers today are very busy.	現在的青少年都很忙碌。
There are many things that we have to do.	有很多事情我們必須去做。
It's not easy being a teenager.	當一個青少年並不容易。
My speech today is about stress.	我今天的演講是關於壓力。
It's something that affects every teen.	這是會影響每位青少年的東西。
Stress in teenagers is a very real problem.	青少年的壓力是一個很大的問題。

7

** ────────────────

stress〔strɛs〕*n.* 壓力　　teenager〔'tin͵edʒɚ〕*n.* 青少年

today〔tə'de〕*adv.* 現在　　busy〔'bɪzɪ〕*adj.* 忙碌的

easy〔'izɪ〕*adj.* 容易的　　affect〔ə'fɛkt〕*v.* 影響

teen〔tin〕*n.* 青少年（= *teenager*）　　real〔'riəl〕*adj.* 非同小可的

problem〔'prɑbləm〕*n.* 問題　　*a real problem* 一個大問題

First, what is stress?
It is worry or strain caused by
　something new or difficult.
We can get stress from many
　things.

We can feel stressed before a
　test.
We can feel stressed seeing a
　doctor.
We can even feel stressed giving
　a speech!

Teens have a lot of schoolwork to do.
Teens have many exams to prepare
　for.
Teens today are especially stressed.

首先，什麼是壓力？
它是由新的事物或困難的
事情所引起的擔心或緊張。
我們可能會因為很多事情
感到有壓力。

我們可能會在考試前感到
有壓力。
我們可能會因為去看醫生
而感到有壓力。
我們甚至可能會因為發表
演說而感到有壓力！

青少年有很多功課要做。
青少年有很多考試要準
備。
現在的青少年特別有壓力。

＊＊

worry〔ˋwɝɪ〕*n.* 擔心　　strain〔stren〕*n.* 緊張；壓力
cause〔kɔz〕*v.* 引起　　new〔nju〕*adj.* 新的
difficult〔ˋdɪfəˏkʌlt〕*adj.* 困難的
stressed〔strɛst〕*adj.* 感到有壓力的　　test〔tɛst〕*n.* 測驗
doctor〔ˋdɑktɚ〕*n.* 醫生　　*see a doctor* 看醫生
give a speech 發表演說　　schoolwork〔ˋskulˏwɝk〕*n.* 學校作業
exam〔ɪgˋzæm〕*n.* 考試　　prepare〔prɪˋpɛr〕*v.* 準備
especially〔əˋspɛʃəlɪ〕*adv.* 特別地

So, what can stress do to teenagers?

那麼，壓力會對青少年產生什麼影響？

The effects of stress are many.

壓力帶來的影響有很多。

Every teenager handles stress differently.

每個青少年會以不同的方式應付壓力。

Some teens cry a lot.

有些青少年會常哭。

Some teens feel bad about themselves.

有些青少年會覺得自己不夠好。

Others can even get angry.

有些甚至可能會生氣。

Stress is powerful.

壓力是強而有力的。

Stress can affect our emotions.

壓力可能會影響我們的情緒。

It makes teenagers feel depressed.

它會讓青少年覺得沮喪。

7

** ——————————————————

effect〔ɪˈfɛkt〕*n.* 影響

handle〔ˈhændl̩〕*v.* 處理；應付

differently〔ˈdɪfərəntlɪ〕*adv.* 不同地；以不同的方式

cry〔kraɪ〕*v.* 哭　　***a lot*** 常常　　bad〔bæd〕*adj.* 不好的

others〔ˈʌðəz〕*pron.* 其他人　　angry〔ˈæŋgrɪ〕*adj.* 生氣的

powerful〔ˈpauəfəl〕*adj.* 強有力的

emotion〔ɪˈmoʃən〕*n.* 情緒　　depressed〔dɪˈprɛst〕*adj.* 沮喪的

Stress can also affect our bodies.　壓力也會影響我們的身體。

Many effects can be either seen
　or felt.　許多影響可以看得到或感覺
得到。

Here are some danger signs.　這裡有一些危險的徵兆。

Our palms may start to sweat.　我們的手心可能會開始出汗。

We could feel butterflies in our
　stomachs.　我們可能會感到緊張。

Our hearts may start beating faster.　我們可能會開始心跳加快。

Some teens may start to have
　headaches.　有些青少年可能會開始頭
痛。

Others may even break out in rashes.　有些人甚至可能會出疹子。

Teens have to be aware of these
　symptoms.　青少年必須注意這些症狀。

** ————————————————————

body〔'badɪ〕 *n.* 身體　　*either…or~*　…或~

danger〔'dendʒə 〕 *n.* 危險　　sign〔saɪn〕 *n.* 信號；徵兆

palm〔pɑm〕 *n.* 手掌；手心　　start〔stɑrt〕 *v.* 開始

sweat〔swɛt〕 *v.* 流汗　　butterflies〔'bʌtə,flaɪz〕 *n. pl.* 緊張

stomach〔'stʌmək〕 *n.* 胃

feel butterflies in one's stomach 感到緊張

beat〔bit〕 *v.* 跳動　　fast〔fæst〕 *adv.* 快速地

headache〔'hɛd,ek〕 *n.* 頭痛　　*break out* 發出；突然被佈滿 *< in >*

rash〔ræʃ〕 *n.* 疹子　　aware〔ə'wɛr〕 *adj.* 知道的；察覺到的

be aware of 知道；察覺到　　symptom〔'sɪmptəm〕 *n.* 症狀

So**, **what can teenagers do about stress?	那麼，青少年要如何處理壓力呢？
There are many things we can do.	有許多我們可以做的事。
Here are some tips.	這裡有一些建議。
We can train ourselves to relax.	我們可以訓練自己放鬆。
We can try to get enough sleep every night.	我們可以試著每晚有足夠的睡眠。
We can talk to people that we trust.	我們可以和信任的人談一談。
Most of all, we can try not to get upset over things we can't change.	最重要的是，我們可以試著不要為了自己無法改變的事情而苦惱。
Sometimes bad things happen to us.	有時候，不好的事情發生在我們身上。
We just have to grin and bear it.	我們只能逆來順受。

7

✽✽ ────────────

tip〔tɪp〕*n.* 建議　　train〔tren〕*v.* 訓練
ourselves〔aʊr'sɛlvz〕*pron.* 我們自己
relax〔rɪ'læks〕*v.* 放鬆　　try〔traɪ〕*v.* 嘗試
enough〔ɪ'nʌf, ə'nʌf〕*adj.* 足夠的　　trust〔trʌst〕*v.* 信任
most of all 最重要的是（= *most important of all*）
upset〔ʌp'sɛt〕*adj.* 心煩的；苦惱的　　change〔tʃendʒ〕*v.* 改變
happen〔'hæpən〕*v.* 發生　　grin〔grɪn〕*v.* 露齒而笑
bear〔bɛr〕*v.* 忍受　　***grin and bear it*** 苦笑著忍受；逆來順受

Stress is everywhere.	壓力無所不在。
It is a part of our everyday lives.	它是我們日常生活的一部分。
We can't escape it.	我們逃離不了它。
But stress isn't always a bad thing.	但是壓力不一定是壞事。
Without stress, we would get lazy.	如果沒有壓力,我們會變懶惰。
Without stress, nothing would get done.	如果沒有壓力,就無法完成任何事。
Teenagers shouldn't try to avoid stress.	青少年不該試著逃避壓力。
We should just try to manage it better.	我們應該試著更妥善地處理它。
Take a deep breath and relax!	做個深呼吸,然後放輕鬆!

** ————————————

everywhere〔ˈɛvrɪˌhwɛr〕*adv.* 到處   part〔pɑrt〕*n.* 部分

everyday〔ˈɛvrɪˈde〕*adj.* 日常的   escape〔əˈskep〕*v.* 逃離

not always 未必;不一定   without〔wɪðˈaʊt〕*prep.* 沒有

lazy〔ˈlezɪ〕*adj.* 懶惰的   done〔dʌn〕*adj.* 完成的

avoid〔əˈvɔɪd〕*v.* 避免;逃避

manage〔ˈmænɪdʒ〕*v.* 管理;處理

better〔ˈbɛtɚ〕*adv.* 更好地

deep〔dip〕*adj.* 深的

breath〔brɛθ〕*n.* 呼吸

take a deep breath 做個深呼吸

📋 背景說明

　　青少年的壓力不外乎就是升學。很多人只知道唸書，一遇到挫折，就覺得像是世界末日來臨，嚴重的甚至還會自殺。大家在強調成績、名校之餘，應該要教導青少年如何紓解壓力。

1. ***Stress in teenagers is a very real problem.***

stress〔strɛs〕*n.* 壓力　　teenager〔ˈtinˌedʒɚ〕*n.* 青少年
real〔ˈriəl〕*adj.* 非同小可的　　problem〔ˈprɑbləm〕*n.* 問題
a real problem 一個大問題

　　real 的基本意思是「真的」，在此是作「非同小可的」解。這句話的意思是「青少年的壓力是一個很大的問題。」也可說成：

Many teenagers suffer from stress.
（許多青少年因壓力而受苦。）

Stress causes problems for many teens.
（壓力給許多青少年帶來問題。）

Stress among teens is an important issue.
（在青少年之間的壓力是一個很重要的問題。）

suffer〔ˈsʌfɚ〕*v.* 受苦　　cause〔kɔz〕*v.* 造成
teen〔tin〕*n.* 青少年（*= teenager*）
among〔əˈmʌŋ〕*prep.* 在…之間
important〔ɪmˈpɔrtn̩t〕*adj.* 重要的
issue〔ˈɪʃʊ〕*n.* 議題；問題

7

2. *Every teenager handles stress differently.*

handle〔'hændḷ〕*v.* 處理；應付

differently〔'dɪfərəntlɪ〕*adv.* 不同地；以不同的方式

　　這句話的意思是「每個青少年會用不同的方式應付壓力。」也可說成：

Every teen copes with stress in a different
　way.（每個青少年會用不同的方式應付壓力。）

How teens deal with stress varies from
　person to person.
（青少年應付壓力的方式會因人而異。）

All teenagers manage stress in their own way.
（所有的青少年都會用自己的方式應付壓力。）

cope with 應付；處理

different〔'dɪfrənt〕*adj.* 不同的

way〔we〕*n.* 方式　　*deal with* 應付；處理

vary〔'vɛrɪ〕*v.* 不同（= *differ*）

manage〔'mænɪdʒ〕*v.* 設法應付

3. *Some teens cry a lot.*

cry〔kraɪ〕*v.* 哭　　*a lot* 常常

　　這句話的意思是「有些青少年會常哭。」也可說成：

Some teenagers frequently break down
　in tears.（有些青少年常常崩潰大哭。）

Some young people spend their days crying
　　about it.
（有些年輕人會整天爲這件事哭泣。）

Some teens often cry when they feel stress.
（當有些青少年感覺到有壓力時，常常會哭。）

frequently〔ˈfrikwəntlɪ〕*adv.* 經常
break down （精神）崩潰　　tear〔tɪr〕*n.* 眼淚
in tears 流著淚；哭泣著　　feel〔fil〕*v.* 感覺到

4. *Many effects can be either seen or felt.*
　　effect〔ɪˈfɛkt〕*n.* 影響　　***either…or~*** …或~

　　　這句話的意思是「許多影響可以看得到或感覺得到。」
也可説成：

Many signs of stress can be seen or felt.
（許多壓力的徵兆可以看得到或感覺得到。）

Many effects of stress are physical.
（許多壓力的影響是身體方面的。）

We can see or feel many of the effects that
　　stress has on us.
（我們可以看到或感覺到壓力對我們的許多影響。）

sign〔saɪn〕*n.* 徵兆
physical〔ˈfɪzɪkl̩〕*adj.* 身體的

7

either…or~「…或~」，其用法舉例如下：

We can go to *either* the movies *or* the
  skating rink.（我們可以去看電影或去溜冰場。）

We can *either* study hard *or* fail the test.
  （我們可以用功讀書或考試不及格。）

We can be *either* an optimist *or* a pessimist.
  （我們可以成為樂觀的人或悲觀的人。）

go to the movies 去看電影　*skating rink* 溜冰場
fail〔fel〕*v.*（考試）不及格
test〔tɛst〕*n.* 測驗
optimist〔'ɑptəmɪst〕*n.* 樂觀者
pessimist〔'pɛsəmɪst〕*n.* 悲觀者

5. *Here are some danger signs.*

  danger〔'dendʒɚ〕*n.* 危險　　sign〔saɪn〕*n.* 徵兆

  這句話的意思是「這裡有一些危險的徵兆。」也可說成：

  Here are some warning signs.
    （這裡有一些警告的徵兆。）

  Here are some things to watch out for.
    （這裡有一些要注意的事。）

  Here are some common symptoms of stress.
    （這裡有一些壓力常見的症狀。）

  warning〔'wɔrnɪŋ〕*adj.* 警告的　*watch out for* 注意
  common〔'kɑmən〕*adj.* 常見的
  symptom〔'sɪmptəm〕*n.* 症狀

6. ***We could feel butterflies in our stomachs.***

butterflies〔ˈbʌtɚˌflaɪz〕*n. pl.* 緊張

stomach〔ˈstʌmək〕*n.* 胃

feel butterflies in *one's* ***stomach***　感到緊張

> butterfly 的基本意思是「蝴蝶」，在此是作「緊張」解，要用複數。這句話的意思是「我們可能會感到緊張。」也可說成：

> We could feel nervous.（我們可能會覺得緊張。）
>
> We could feel anxious.（我們可能會覺得焦慮。）
>
> We could feel uneasy.（我們可能會覺得不安。）

> nervous〔ˈnɝvəs〕*adj.* 緊張的
>
> anxious〔ˈæŋkʃəs〕*adj.* 焦慮的
>
> uneasy〔ʌnˈizɪ〕*adj.* 不安的

7. ***Others may even break out in rashes.***

break out 發出；突然被佈滿 < *in* >　　rash〔ræʃ〕*n.* 疹子

> 這句話的意思是「有些人甚至可能會出疹子。」也可說成：

> Others may develop a rash.
>
> （有些人可能會出現疹子。）
>
> Other teens may have skin problems.
>
> （有些青少年可能會有皮膚上的問題。）
>
> Others may experience hives.（有些人可能有蕁麻疹。）

> develop〔dɪˈvɛləp〕*v.* 顯現出　　skin〔skɪn〕*adj.* 皮膚的
>
> experience〔ɪkˈspɪrɪəns〕*v.* 經歷
>
> hives〔haɪvz〕*n. pl.* 蕁麻疹

7

另外，***break out*** 除了作「發出；突然被佈滿」解外，還有其他意思，例如：

① 作「（火災、戰爭、疾病的）爆發；突然發生」解。

A fire ***broke out*** last night.（昨天晚上發生了火災。）

Flu has ***broken out*** all over the district.

（流行性感冒已經在整個地區蔓延開來。）

They got married a month before the war ***broke out***.

（他們在戰爭爆發前一個月結婚。）

② 作「逃走」解。

Two prisoners ***broke out*** of jail last night.

（昨晚有兩個囚犯越獄。）

flu〔flu〕*n.* 流行性感冒（= *influenza*〔ˌɪnfluˈɛnzə〕）
all over 遍及　　district〔ˈdɪstrɪkt〕*n.* 地區
prisoner〔ˈprɪzn̩ə˞〕*n.* 囚犯　　jail〔dʒel〕*n.* 監獄

8. ***Here are some tips.***

tip〔tɪp〕*n.* 建議

tip 的基本意思是「尖端」，在此是作「建議」解。
這句話的意思是「這裡有一些建議。」也可說成：

Here are some suggestions.（這裡有一些建議。）
Here is some advice.（這裡有一些建議。）
Here are some things that you can do.

（這裡有一些你可以做的事。）

suggestion〔səgˈdʒɛstʃən〕*n.* 建議
advice〔ədˈvaɪs〕*n.* 建議；勸告

9. *Most of all, we can try not to get upset over things we can't change.*

   most of all 最重要的是（ = *most important of all* ）
   upset〔ʌpˈsɛt〕*adj.* 心煩的；苦惱的
   change〔tʃendʒ〕*v.* 改變

   　　這句話的意思是「最重要的是，我們可以試著不要爲了自己無法改變的事情而苦惱。」也可說成：

   Most of all, we should try to stay calm when we can't change the situation.
   （最重要的是，當我們無法改變情況時，我們應該設法保持冷靜。）

   Most of all, we shouldn't let things we can't change bother us. （最重要的是，我們不應該讓自己無法改變的事情困擾我們。）

   Most of all, we shouldn't be disturbed by things we can't control. （最重要的是，我們不應該被自己無法控制的事情擾亂。）

   stay〔ste〕*v.* 保持　　calm〔kɑm〕*adj.* 冷靜的
   situation〔ˌsɪtʃuˈeʃən〕*n.* 情況　　bother〔ˈbɑðɚ〕*v.* 困擾
   disturb〔dɪˈstɝb〕*v.* 擾亂　　control〔kənˈtrol〕*v.* 控制

7

10. *We just have to grin and bear it.*

    grin〔grɪn〕*v.* 露齒而笑　　bear〔bɛr〕*v.* 忍受
    grin and bear it 苦笑著忍受；逆來順受

    　　這句話字面的意思是「我們只要笑一笑，忍過去就好了。」引申爲「我們只能逆來順受。」也可說成：

We just have to accept the situation.
（我們只要忍受這個情況。）

We just have to make the best of it.
（我們只要在不利的情況下盡力而為。）

We just have to get on with it and not complain.
（我們只要繼續做下去，不要抱怨。）

accept〔 ək'sɛpt 〕v. 接受；忍受
make the best of it 在不利的情況下盡力而為
get on with it 繼續做（ = *continue with what we are doing* ）
complain〔 kəm'plen 〕v. 抱怨

11. ***Without stress, nothing would get done.***

without〔 wɪð'aʊt 〕*prep.* 沒有　　done〔 dʌn 〕*adj.* 完成的

　　　　這句話的意思是「如果沒有壓力，就無法完成任何事。」也可說成：

If there were no stress, people would get lazy.
（如果沒有壓力，人們會變懶惰。）

Without stress, we wouldn't accomplish anything.
（如果沒有壓力，我們不會完成任何事情。）

Without a little pressure, nothing would get
　　finished.（如果沒有一點壓力，沒有事情會完成。）

lazy〔 'lezɪ 〕*adj.* 懶惰的
accomplish〔 ə'kɑmplɪʃ 〕v. 完成　　***a little*** 一點
pressure〔 'prɛʃɚ 〕*n.* 壓力　　finish〔 'fɪnɪʃ 〕v. 完成

 作文範例

Stress in Teenagers

Today's teenagers are very busy people. There are many things that they have to do, and their hectic lifestyle often makes them feel worried. *In fact*, this feeling is stress, and it can be a serious problem.

In order to handle their stress, teenagers must first learn how to recognize it and then know how to reduce it. *First of all*, they have to be aware of the symptoms of stress. These include sweaty palms, a fast heartbeat, crying spells and even uncontrolled anger. If they often experience these symptoms, they should take some steps to alleviate them. *For example*, they can get more sleep and talk to people they trust about their feelings.

Stress is an unavoidable part of nearly everyone's life. *However*, it is something that we can learn to recognize and treat. This is especially important for teenagers. They have to know that bad things happen to everyone, but it is not worth getting upset over every problem.

7

📖 中文翻譯

青少年的壓力

　　現在的青少年非常忙碌。有許多他們必須做的事情，而他們極忙碌的生活方式常讓他們感到憂慮。事實上，這種感覺就是壓力，而它可能是個嚴重的問題。

　　為了應付自己的壓力，青少年必須先學會如何認出它，然後就要知道如何才能減低它。首先，他們必須知道壓力的徵兆。這包括了手汗、心跳加快、持續哭泣，甚至無法控制怒氣。如果他們常常有這些症狀，他們就應該採取一些措施來減輕它們。比如說，他們可以多睡覺，並且向信賴的人談論自己的感受。

　　壓力幾乎是每個人生活中無法避免的一部分。然而，它是那種我們可以學著去認出和治療的東西。這對青少年而言尤其重要。他們必須了解，不好的事情都會發生在每個人身上，但為了問題而苦惱是不值得的。

8. *A Letter to the Principal*

Hello, ladies and gentlemen.
Thanks for taking the time today to listen.
I hope that you will enjoy my speech.

I really like going to school.
Sure it gets hard sometimes.
But school can be really fun, too.

The other day, I decided to write a letter.
This letter was to our school's principal.
Here's what it said.

8

letter (ˈlɛtɚ)
take (tek)
go to school
get (gɛt)
sometimes (ˈsʌmˌtaɪmz)
the other day
say (se)

principal (ˈprɪnsəpḷ)
school (skul)
sure (ʃur)
hard (hɑrd)
fun (fʌn)
decide (dɪˈsaɪd)

Dear Principal Lee,

How are you?

Are you busy?

I'm sorry to bother you.

I know you have a lot to do.

But there's something that I want

to say.

I'm writing you this letter to thank you.

I think people don't often thank you.

But there are many things I'm

thankful for.

---

dear〔dɪr〕   busy〔'bɪzɪ〕

sorry〔'sɔrɪ〕   bother〔'bɑðɚ〕

write *sb.* **a letter**

thankful〔'θæŋkfəl〕

Thank you for my teachers.

My teachers take care of me
   every day.

They teach me about many things.

They teach me math.

They teach me English.

They even teach me science.

My teachers are very smart.

They seem to know everything.

I hope I will be as wise as them
   someday.

8

teacher (ˈtitʃɚ)

teach (titʃ)

science (ˈsaɪəns)

seem (sim)

as···as~

someday (ˈsʌmˌde)

take care of

math (mæθ)

smart (smɑrt)

hope (hop)

wise (waɪz)

Also, thank you for all of the students.

I've made so many good friends here.

We have a great time together.

We have lunch together.

We study together.

We sometimes even go on trips together.

I cherish each of my friendships.

I'll never forget my friends.

They will be in my heart always.

--- ---

make friends	***have a great time***
have〔hæv〕	lunch〔lʌntʃ〕
study〔'stʌdɪ〕	trip〔trɪp〕
go on a trip	cherish〔'tʃɛrɪʃ〕
friendship〔'frɛndʃɪp〕	never〔'nɛvɚ〕
forget〔fɚ'gɛt〕	heart〔hɑrt〕
always〔'ɔlwez〕	

Finally, *thank you for the school*.

Learning is so important.

School is where learning happens.

I learn how to be responsible.

I learn about discipline.

I get wiser day by day.

School prepares me for life.

There are many lessons to learn.

I think my school is the best.

---

finally (ˈfaɪnḷɪ)	learning (ˈlɜnɪŋ)
important (ɪmˈpɔrtṇt)	happen (ˈhæpən)
responsible (rɪˈspɑnsəbḷ)	
discipline (ˈdɪsəplɪn)	*day by day*
prepare (prɪˈpɛr)	life (laɪf)
lesson (ˈlɛsṇ)	

8

In closing*, *it's great to be at
   ***your school*.**
***It has* taught me so much.**
***It has* made me grow up.**

***I'll keep* studying hard.**
***I'll keep* trying my best.**
I won't let myself get lazy.

***School is such a special time*.**
***Junior high only comes once*.**
I will try to make the most of it!

------------------------------- ------

closing (ˈklozɪŋ)	great (gret)
grow up	keep (kip)
try one's best	myself (maɪˈsɛlf)
lazy (ˈlezɪ)	special (ˈspɛʃəl)
junior high	come (kʌm)
once (wʌns)	***make the most of***

8. A Letter to the Principal

🔊 演講解說

Hello, ladies and gentlemen.	哈囉，各位先生，各位女士。
Thanks for taking the time today to listen.	謝謝你們今天花時間聆聽。
I hope that you will enjoy my speech.	我希望你們會喜歡我的演講。
I really like going to school.	我真的很喜歡上學。
Sure it gets hard sometimes.	當然上學有時會很辛苦。
But school can be really fun, too.	但學校也可能很有趣。
The other day, I decided to write a letter.	前幾天，我決定寫一封信。
This letter was to our school's principal.	這封信是要給我們學校的校長。
Here's what it said.	以下是信裡所寫的內容。

8

** ———————————————

letter〔ˈlɛtɚ〕 *n.* 信　　principal〔ˈprɪnsəpḷ〕 *n.* 校長
take〔tek〕 *v.* 花費（時間）　　school〔skul〕 *n.* 學校；上學
go to school 上學　　sure〔ʃʊr〕 *adv.* 當然　*adj.* 確信的
get〔gɛt〕 *v.* 變得　　hard〔hɑrd〕 *adj.* 困難的；辛苦的　*adv.* 努力地
sometimes〔ˈsʌmˌtaɪmz〕 *adv.* 有時候　　fun〔fʌn〕 *adj.* 有趣的
the other day 前幾天　　decide〔dɪˈsaɪd〕 *v.* 決定
say〔se〕 *v.*（信上）寫著

Dear Principal Lee,　　　　　　親愛的李校長：

How are you?　　　　　　　　您好嗎？

Are you busy?　　　　　　　　您在忙嗎？

I'm sorry to bother you.　　　　我很抱歉打擾您。

I know you have a lot to do.　　我知道您有很多事要做。

But there's something that I　　但有件事我想要說。
　　want to say.

I'm writing you this letter to　　我寫這封信給您，是為了
　　thank you.　　　　　　　　要感謝您。

I think people don't often　　　我認為大家不常向您道謝。
　　thank you.

But there are many things I'm　　但我要感謝的事有很多。
　　thankful for.

** ————————————————————

dear〔dɪr〕*adj.* 親愛的　　busy〔'bɪzɪ〕*adj.* 忙碌的

sorry〔'sɔrɪ〕*adj.* 抱歉的

bother〔'bɑðɚ〕*v.* 打擾

write sb. a letter 寫一封信給某人

thankful〔'θæŋkfəl〕*adj.* 感謝的

***Thank you for my teachers*.**　　　　　　我要為我的老師而感謝您。

My teachers take care of me　　　　　　我的老師每天照顧我。
　　every day.

They teach me about many things.　　　　他們教我很多事情。

They teach me math.　　　　　　　　他們教我數學。

They teach me English.　　　　　　　他們教我英文。

They even teach me science.　　　　　　　他們甚至教我自然科學。

My teachers are very smart.　　　　　　　我的老師都很聰明。

They seem to know everything.　　　　　　他們似乎知道所有的事情。

I hope I will be as wise as them　　　　　我希望將來有一天能像他
　　someday.　　　　　　　　　　　　　們一樣聰明。

8

＊＊ ───────────────

teacher〔ˋtitʃɚ〕*n.* 老師

take care of 照顧　　teach〔titʃ〕*v.* 教

math〔mæθ〕*n.* 數學　　science〔ˋsaɪəns〕*n.* 自然科學

smart〔smɑrt〕*adj.* 聰明的

seem〔sim〕*v.* 似乎　　hope〔hop〕*v.* 希望

as…as ～　像～一樣…　　wise〔waɪz〕*adj.* 聰明的

someday〔ˋsʌmˏde〕*adv.*（將來）有一天

***Also*, *thank you for all of the students*.**	我也要為所有的學生而感謝您。
I've made so many good friends here.	我在這裡交到很多好朋友。
We have a great time together.	我們在一起玩得很愉快。
We have lunch together.	我們一起吃午餐。
We study together.	我們一起讀書。
We sometimes even go on trips together.	我們有時甚至會一起去旅行。
I cherish each of my friendships.	我珍惜我的每一段友誼。
I'll never forget my friends.	我絕不會忘記我的朋友。
They will be in my heart always.	他們將永遠在我的心中。

∗∗ ──────────────────

make friends 交朋友　　***have a great time*** 玩得很愉快
have〔hæv〕*v.* 吃；喝　　lunch〔lʌntʃ〕*n.* 午餐
study〔'stʌdɪ〕*v.* 讀書；用功　　trip〔trɪp〕*n.* 旅行
go on a trip 去旅行　　cherish〔'tʃɛrɪʃ〕*v.* 珍惜
friendship〔'frɛndʃɪp〕*n.* 友誼　　never〔'nɛvɚ〕*adv.* 絕不
forget〔fɚ'gɛt〕*v.* 忘記　　heart〔hɑrt〕*n.* 心
always〔'ɔlwez〕*adv.* 總是；永遠

***Finally**, **thank you for the school**.*	最後，我要爲這所學校而感謝您。
Learning is so important.	學習是非常重要的。
School is where learning happens.	學校就是學習的地方。
***I learn** how to be responsible.*	我學會如何變得有責任感。
***I learn** about discipline.*	我學會紀律。
I get wiser day by day.	我變得一天比一天聰明。
School prepares me for life.	學校讓我爲生涯做準備。
There are many lessons to learn.	有很多的課程可以學習。
I think my school is the best.	我認爲我的學校是最棒的。

** ——————————————————

finally〔ˈfaɪnḷɪ〕*adv.* 最後　　learning〔ˈlɜnɪŋ〕*n.* 學習

important〔ɪmˈpɔrtṇt〕*adj.* 重要的

happen〔ˈhæpən〕*v.* 發生

responsible〔rɪˈspɑnsəbḷ〕*adj.* 有責任感的

discipline〔ˈdɪsəplɪn〕*n.* 紀律

day by day 逐日；一天天地

prepare〔prɪˈpɛr〕*v.* 使做準備

life〔laɪf〕*n.* 生涯　　lesson〔ˈlɛsṇ〕*n.* 課程

8

***In closing**, it's great to be at your school.*	總之，能在您的學校真是太棒了。
It has taught me so much.	它教了我很多。
It has made me grow up.	它使我成長。
I'll keep studying hard.	我會持續努力用功。
I'll keep trying my best.	我會持續盡全力。
I won't let myself get lazy.	我不會讓我自己怠惰。
School is such a special time.	上學是一段很特別的時光。
Junior high only comes once.	國中只有一次。
I will try to make the most of it!	我會試著充分利用它！

** ——————————————

closing〔'klozɪŋ〕*n.* （演講或書信的）結尾；結束

great〔gret〕*adj.* 很棒的　　***grow up*** 長大；成長

keep〔kip〕*v.* 持續　　***try one's best*** 盡全力

myself〔maɪ'sɛlf〕*pron.* 我自己

lazy〔'lezɪ〕*adj.* 懶惰的　　special〔'spɛʃəl〕*adj.* 特別的

junior high 國中　　come〔kʌm〕*v.* 來臨；出現

once〔wʌns〕*adv.* 一次　　***make the most of*** 充分利用

📖 背景說明

　　學校是讓學生學習的地方，除了學習技能，也學習人與人之間的互動。爲了提供學生安全舒適的學習環境，從師資團隊到環境設施，都要經過不斷的改善。能有這一切，必須感謝校長的領導和付出。

1. ***Sure it gets hard sometimes.***

sure〔ʃur〕*adv.* 當然　　get〔gɛt〕*v.* 變得
hard〔hɑrd〕*adj.* 困難的；辛苦的

　　這句話字面的意思是「當然它有時會變得很辛苦。」在此引申爲「當然上學有時會很辛苦。」也可說成：

Of course, it's hard at times.

（當然，上學有時會很辛苦。）

Yes, it's difficult sometimes.

（是的，上學有時會很辛苦。）

Naturally it's not always easy.

（當然上學未必是輕鬆的。）

of course 當然　　***at times*** 有時候
difficult〔ˈdɪfəˌkʌlt〕*adj.* 困難的；辛苦的
naturally〔ˈnætʃərəlɪ〕*adv.* 當然
not always 未必
easy〔ˈizɪ〕*adj.* 容易的；輕鬆的

8

2. ***The other day, I decided to write a letter.***

the other day 前幾天　　decide〔dɪˈsaɪd〕*v.* 決定

　　the other day 是作「前幾天」解，這句話的意思是「幾天前，我決定寫一封信。」也可說成：

A few days ago, I wrote a letter.
（幾天前，我寫了一封信。）

Not long ago, I made the decision to write
a letter.（不久前，我決定寫一封信。）

【decision〔dɪˈsɪʒən〕*n.* 決定】

3. ***I hope I will be as wise as them someday.***

hope〔hop〕*v.* 希望　　wise〔waɪz〕*adj.* 聰明的
someday〔ˈsʌmˌde〕*adv.*（將來）有一天

　　someday 只能表示「將來的某一天」，而 one day
則可指「將來或過去的某一天」。這句話的意思是「我
希望我將來有一天能像他們一樣聰明。」也可說成：

I hope I will be as sensible as they are in the
future.（我希望我將來能像他們一樣明智。）

I hope I can be as smart as them.
（我希望我能像他們一樣聰明。）

I hope that I will turn out as intelligent as
they are.（我希望我將會變得和他們一樣聰明。）

sensible〔ˈsɛnsəb!〕*adj.* 明智的　　*in the future* 將來
smart〔smɑrt〕*adj.* 聰明的　　*turn out* 最後成為
intelligent〔ɪnˈtɛlədʒənt〕*adj.* 聰明的

4. ***We sometimes even go on trips together.***

sometimes〔ˈsʌmˌtaɪmz〕*adv.* 有時候

trip〔trɪp〕*n.* 旅行　　***go on a trip*** 去旅行

　　　　這句話的意思是「我們有時甚至會一起去旅行。」
也可説成：

Sometimes we even take a trip together.

（我們有時甚至會一起去旅行。）

Sometimes we even travel together.

（我們有時甚至會一起去旅行。）

Sometimes we even go someplace together.

（我們有時甚至會一起去某個地方。）

take a trip 去旅行　　travel〔ˈtrævl̩〕*v.* 旅行
someplace〔ˈsʌmˌples〕*adv.* 到某處

5. ***School is where learning happens.***

learning〔ˈlɜnɪŋ〕*n.* 學習　　happen〔ˈhæpən〕*v.* 發生

　　　　這句話字面的意思是「學校是學習會發生的地方。」
引申爲「學校就是學習的地方。」也可説成：

School is where we learn.

（學校是我們學習的地方。）

If we want to learn, we must go to school.

（如果我們想學習，我們必須上學。）

School is the place to learn.

（學校是學習的地方。）

8

6. *I get wiser day by day.*

wise〔waɪz〕*adj.* 聰明的　　***day by day*** 逐日；一天天

　　　　這句話的意思是「我變得一天比一天聰明。」也可說成：

　　　　　　　　My wisdom gradually grows.

　　　　　　　　（我的智慧逐漸增長。）

　　　　　　　　I learn a little bit every day.

　　　　　　　　（我每天都學到一點東西。）

　　　　　　　　My common sense constantly grows.

　　　　　　　　（我的常識不斷地增長。）

　　　　　　　　wisdom〔'wɪzdəm〕*n.* 智慧
　　　　　　　　gradually〔'grædʒuəlɪ〕*adv.* 逐漸地
　　　　　　　　grow〔gro〕*v.* 增長
　　　　　　　　a little bit 一點點　　***common sense*** 常識
　　　　　　　　constantly〔'kɑnstəntlɪ〕*adv.* 不斷地

7. *School prepares me for life.*

prepare〔prɪ'pɛr〕*v.* 使做準備
life〔laɪf〕*n.* 生涯

　　　　prepare sb. for 是作「使某人做⋯的準備」解，所以這句話的意思是「學校讓我爲生涯做準備。」也可說成：

School gets me ready for adulthood.
（學校讓我爲成年做好準備。）

School equips me for the real world.
（學校讓我準備好面對現實的世界。）

School readies me for what will come next.
（學校讓我爲接下來會發生的事做好準備。）

ready〔ˈrɛdɪ〕*adj.* 準備好的　*v.* 使準備好 < *for* >
adulthood〔əˈdʌlthʊd〕*n.* 成年
equip〔ɪˈkwɪp〕*v.* 使有準備 < *for* >
real〔ˈriəl〕*adj.* 現實的
come〔kʌm〕*v.* 出現　　next〔nɛkst〕*adv.* 接著

8. *In closing, it's great to be at your school.*
closing〔ˈklozɪŋ〕*n.*（演講或書信的）結尾；結束

　　這句話的意思是「總之，能在您的學校眞是太棒了。」也可說成：

Finally, it's a pleasure to be a student here.
（最後，很高興能成爲這裡的學生。）

The last thing I want to say is that I enjoy
　being at your school.
（最後，我想說的是我喜歡在您的學校。）

Lastly, I'm very happy to be a student here.
（最後，我很高興能成爲這裡的學生。）

finally〔ˈfaɪnḷɪ〕*adv.* 最後　　pleasure〔ˈplɛʒɚ〕*n.* 高興的事
the last thing 最後　　enjoy〔ɪnˈdʒɔɪ〕*v.* 喜歡
lastly〔ˈlæstlɪ〕*adv.* 最後

8

9. *I will try to make the most of it!*
   try〔traɪ〕*v.* 試著
   make the most of 充分利用

> *make the most of* 字面的意思是「製造最多的」，引申為「充分利用」。這句話的意思是「我會試著充分利用它！」也可說成：

> I'll try to get everything I can out of it.
> （我會試著儘可能從那裡得到一切。）

> I'll try to take full advantage of it.
> （我會試著充分利用它。）

> I'll make the most of the opportunity.
> （我會充分利用這個機會。）

> *out of* 從⋯   *take advantage of* 利用
> full〔fʊl〕*adj.* 充分的
> opportunity〔͵ɑpɚ'tjunətɪ〕*n.* 機會

 作文範例

A Letter to the Principal

Dear Principal Lee,

I'm writing this letter to thank you. ***In fact***, there are many things that I want to thank you for. ***First of all***, I am grateful for my teachers. They take care of me every day, and they teach me many things. They are so smart that they seem to know everything. I hope that I will be as wise as them someday.

I'd also like to thank you for all of the students and the school itself. I've made a lot of good friends here. I'm sure that I will never forget them. From the school, I have learned important values. I have developed responsibility and discipline. ***In short***, this school is preparing me for life.

In closing, it's great to be at your school. It has taught me so much and has made me grow up. I'll keep studying hard and trying my best. I'll try to make the most of my time in junior high!

Sincerely,

Amy Lin

8

📖 中文翻譯

給校長的一封信

親愛的李校長：

　　我寫這封信是為了要感謝您。事實上，我想感謝您的事有很多。首先，我要為我的老師而感激您。他們每天照顧我，並教我很多事情。他們聰明得似乎知道所有的事情。我希望將來有一天能像他們一樣聰明。

　　我也想要為所有學生，和學校本身而感謝您。我在這裡交了很多好朋友。我確信我絕不會忘記他們。從這所學校，我學到重要的價值觀。我培養了責任感和紀律。簡言之，這所學校讓我為生涯做準備。

　　最後，能在您的學校就讀真是太棒了。它教了我很多，並使我成長。我會持續努力用功和盡全力。我會試著充分利用我的國中時光！

林愛咪　敬上

9. *An Unforgettable Gift*

***Welcome**, and please be seated.*

I am going to tell a story now.

Let's get started.

Getting gifts is a lot of fun.

It's always a big surprise!

There was one gift that I will never forget.

Today, I'd like to tell you about it.

I hope you enjoy my story.

It is a story about an unforgettable gift.

unforgettable〔͵ʌnfɚˋgɛtəbḷ〕

gift〔gɪft〕 welcome〔ˋwɛlkəm〕

seat〔sit〕 *be seated*

story〔ˋstorɪ〕 start〔stɑrt〕

get started surprise〔səˋpraɪz〕

forget〔fɚˋgɛt〕 enjoy〔ɪnˋdʒɔɪ〕

9

It was my eleventh birthday.

My parents threw me a party.

All of my friends were there to

　celebrate.

We sang songs.

We ate birthday cake.

It was a wonderful time.

Later on, it was time for gifts.

My parents had promised me a big one.

I was so excited!

----

eleventh〔ɪ'lɛvənθ〕　　birthday〔'bɝθ,de〕

parents〔'pɛrənts〕　　throw〔θro〕

party〔'pɑrtɪ〕　　***throw** sb. **a party***

celebrate〔'sɛlə,bret〕　　sing〔sɪŋ〕

song〔sɔŋ〕　　wonderful〔'wʌndəfəl〕

later on　　promise〔'prɑmɪs〕

excited〔ɪk'saɪtɪd〕

My mom brought out a big present.
It was wrapped in white paper.
There was a big red bow on top.

Mom placed it on the table.
She told me to be careful with it.
I couldn't wait to open it!

There were holes on the side of
   the box.
I wondered what was inside!
I quickly unwrapped the package.

---

bring out

wrap (ræp)

on top

careful (ˈkɛrfəl)

hole (hol)

wonder (ˈwʌndɚ)

quickly (ˈkwɪklɪ)

package (ˈpækɪdʒ)

present (ˈprɛzn̩t)

bow (bo)

place (ples)

wait (wet)

side (saɪd)

inside (ˈɪnˈsaɪd)

unwrap (ʌnˈræp)

9

Inside the box was a puppy!

I was so surprised!

It was so cute!

The dog kept barking at me.

Its tail wagged nonstop.

It jumped up and licked my face.

I couldn't help but laugh.

I thanked my mom and dad.

It was the best present ever!

---

inside (ɪn'saɪd)

so (so)

cute (kjut)

bark (bɑrk)

wag (wæg)

jump (dʒʌmp)

cannot help but + *V.*

ever ('ɛvɚ)

puppy ('pʌpɪ)

surprised (sə'praɪzd)

keep (kip)

tail (tel)

nonstop ('nɑn'stɑp)

lick (lɪk)

laugh (læf)

I decided to name him Rover.

Rover is a very playful dog.

He loves to play fetch.

I take him for walks in the park.

Rover likes to be around other dogs.

I think they like Rover, too.

I help him take baths.

I feed Rover every day.

Rover is a big part of my life.

---

decide (dɪ'saɪd)

playful ('plefəl)

walk (wɔk)

park (pɑrk)

take a bath

big (bɪg)

life (laɪf)

name (nem)

fetch (fɛtʃ)

take ~ for a walk

around (ə'raʊnd)

feed (fid)

part (pɑrt)

9

Rover was an unforgettable present.

He is so much more than a birthday
  gift.

He is my best friend.

He was the best present my parents
  ever gave me.

I'll never forget my eleventh birthday.

It was the day Rover joined our family.

Gifts can brighten a person's day.

Some gifts can even change
  people's lives.

Show your kindness with a gift!

---

more than	join 〔 dʒɔɪn 〕
brighten 〔'braɪtn̩ 〕	person 〔'pɝsn̩ 〕
show 〔 ʃo 〕	kindness 〔'kaɪndnɪs 〕

9. An Unforgettable Gift

演講解說

***Welcome**, and please **be seated**.*	歡迎，請坐。
I am going to tell a story now.	我現在要說一個故事。
*Let's **get started**.*	我們開始吧。
Getting gifts is a lot of fun.	收到禮物是很有趣的。
It's always a big surprise!	它總是令人十分驚奇！
There was one gift that I will never forget.	有一份禮物我絕不會忘記。
Today, I'd like to tell you about it.	今天，我想要告訴你們有關它的事。
I hope you enjoy my story.	我希望你們會喜歡我的故事。
It is a story about an unforgettable gift.	這是一個關於一份難忘的禮物的故事。

** ──────────

unforgettable〔͵ʌnfɚˋɡɛtəbḷ〕*adj.* 難忘的　　gift〔ɡɪft〕*n.* 禮物
welcome〔ˋwɛlkəm〕*interj.* 歡迎　　seat〔sit〕*v.* 使坐下；使就座
be seated 坐下　　story〔ˋstorɪ〕*n.* 故事　　start〔stɑrt〕*v.* 開始
get started 開始　　surprise〔səˋpraɪz〕*n.* 驚奇
forget〔fɚˋɡɛt〕*v.* 忘記　　enjoy〔ɪnˋdʒɔɪ〕*v.* 喜歡

9

It was my eleventh birthday.	那是我十一歲的生日。
My parents threw me a party.	我的父母爲我舉行派對。
All of my friends were there to celebrate.	我所有的朋友都有來慶祝。
We sang songs.	我們唱歌。
We ate birthday cake.	我們吃生日蛋糕。
It was a wonderful time.	那是一段很棒的時光。
Later on, it was time for gifts.	後來，拆禮物的時間到了。
My parents had promised me a big one.	我的父母答應會給我一份大禮。
I was so excited!	我非常興奮！

** ───────────────

eleventh〔ɪˋlɛvənθ〕*adj.* 第十一的

birthday〔ˋbɝθ‚de〕*n.* 生日　　parents〔ˋpɛrənts〕*n. pl.* 父母

throw〔θro〕*v.* 舉行　　party〔ˋpɑrtɪ〕*n.* 派對

throw sb. a party 爲某人舉行派對（= *throw a party for sb.*）

celebrate〔ˋsɛlə‚bret〕*v.* 慶祝　　sing〔sɪŋ〕*v.* 唱

song〔sɔŋ〕*n.* 歌曲

wonderful〔ˋwʌndəfəl〕*adj.* 極好的；很棒的

later on 後來　　promise〔ˋprɑmɪs〕*v.* 答應

excited〔ɪkˋsaɪtɪd〕*adj.* 興奮的

My mom brought out a big present.	我媽拿出一個大禮物。
It was wrapped in white paper.	它用白色的紙包著。
There was a big red bow on top.	上面有一個紅色的大蝴蝶結。
Mom placed it on the table.	媽媽把它放在桌上。
She told me to be careful with it.	她告訴我要小心對待它。
I couldn't wait to open it!	我等不及要打開它！
There were holes on the side of the box.	盒子的側面有洞。
I wondered what was inside!	我想知道裡面是什麼！
I quickly unwrapped the package.	我很快地打開包裝盒。

＊＊ ————————————

bring out 拿出　　present〔'prɛzn̩t〕*n.* 禮物

wrap〔ræp〕*v.* 包；裹　　bow〔bo〕*n.* 蝴蝶結

on top 在上面　　place〔ples〕*v.* 放置

careful〔'kɛrfəl〕*adj.* 小心的

wait〔wet〕*v.* 等　　hole〔hol〕*n.* 洞

side〔saɪd〕*n.* 側面　　wonder〔'wʌndɚ〕*v.* 想知道

inside〔'ɪn'saɪd〕*adv.* 在裡面

quickly〔'kwɪklɪ〕*adv.* 快速地　　unwrap〔ʌn'ræp〕*v.* 打開

package〔'pækɪdʒ〕*n.* 包裝紙；包裝盒

9

Inside the box was a puppy!
I was so surprised!
It was so cute!

盒子裡面是一隻小狗！
我很驚訝！
牠很可愛！

The dog kept barking at me.
Its tail wagged nonstop.
It jumped up and licked
　my face.

那隻狗一直對著我叫。
牠的尾巴搖個不停。
牠跳起來舔我的臉。

I couldn't help but laugh.
I thanked my mom and dad.
It was the best present ever!

我不禁大笑起來。
我向我的爸媽道謝。
牠是我有生以來最好的禮物！

**　**

inside〔ɪnˈsaɪd〕*prep.* 在…裡面　　puppy〔ˈpʌpɪ〕*n.* 小狗

so〔so〕*adv.* 非常　　surprised〔səˈpraɪzd〕*adj.* 驚訝的

cute〔kjut〕*adj.* 可愛的　　keep〔kip〕*v.* 持續；一直

bark〔bɑrk〕*v.* 吠叫　　tail〔tel〕*n.* 尾巴

wag〔wæg〕*v.* 搖動　　nonstop〔ˈnɑnˈstɑp〕*adv.* 不停地

jump〔dʒʌmp〕*v.* 跳　　lick〔lɪk〕*v.* 舔

***cannot help but* + *V*.** 忍不住…；不禁…

laugh〔læf〕*v.* 笑　　ever〔ˈɛvɚ〕*adv.* 至今

I decided to name him Rover.　　我決定將牠取名爲來福。

Rover is a very playful dog.　　來福是一隻很愛玩的狗。

He loves to play fetch.　　他喜歡玩你丟我撿的遊戲。

I take him for walks in the park.　　我會帶他去公園裡散步。

Rover likes to be around other
dogs.　　來福喜歡在別的狗周圍。

I think they like Rover, too.　　我想牠們也喜歡來福。

I help him take baths.　　我會幫他洗澡。

I feed Rover every day.　　我會每天餵來福。

Rover is a big part of my life.　　來福是我生活中很重要的
一部分。

**　——————————————

decide〔dɪˋsaɪd〕*v.* 決定　　name〔nem〕*v.* 取名

playful〔ˋplefəl〕*adj.* 愛玩的　　fetch〔fɛtʃ〕*n.* 去拿來

walk〔wɔk〕*n.* 散步　　***take ~ for a walk*** 帶~去散步

park〔pɑrk〕*n.* 公園　　around〔əˋraʊnd〕*prep.* 在…周圍

take a bath 洗澡　　feed〔fid〕*v.* 餵

big〔bɪg〕*adj.* 大的；重要的

part〔pɑrt〕*n.* 部分

life〔laɪf〕*n.* 生活；一生

9

Rover was an unforgettable present. 來福是個令人難忘的禮物。

He is so much more than a birthday gift. 他絕不只是個生日禮物。

He is my best friend. 他是我最好的朋友。

He was the best present my parents ever gave me. 他是我的父母給我的最好的禮物。

I'll never forget my eleventh birthday. 我絕不會忘記我的十一歲生日。

It was the day Rover joined our family. 那是來福成為我們家庭成員的日子。

Gifts can brighten a person's day. 禮物可以使人愉快一整天。

Some gifts can even change people's lives. 有些禮物甚至可以改變人的一生。

Show your kindness with a gift! 用禮物來表現你的善意吧！

**

more than 超過；不只是
join〔dʒɔɪn〕*v.* 加入；成為⋯的一員
brighten〔ˈbraɪtn̩〕*v.* 使變亮；使愉快
person〔ˈpɝsn̩〕*n.* 人　　show〔ʃo〕*v.* 表現
kindness〔ˈkaɪndnɪs〕*n.* 親切；善意

背景說明

　　每一份禮物，都是一份心意。禮物的價值，不在於它的價格，而在於它所代表的意義。你是否曾經收過意義重大且令你難忘的禮物呢？試著用英文和大家分享。

1. ***My parents threw me a party.***

parents〔ˈpɛrənts〕*n. pl.* 父母

throw〔θro〕*v.* 舉行

party〔ˈpɑrtɪ〕*n.* 派對

　　throw 的基本意思是「丟」，在此是作「舉行」解。這句話的意思是「我的父母為我舉行派對。」也可說成：

　　　My parents held a party for me.

　　　（我的父母為我舉行派對。）

　　　My parents gave me a party.

　　　（我的父母為我舉行派對。）

　　　My parents celebrated it with a party.

　　　（我的父母舉行派對來慶祝。）

　　　hold〔hold〕*v.* 舉行　　give〔gɪv〕*v.* 舉行
　　　celebrate〔ˈsɛləˌbret〕*v.* 慶祝

9

2. *Later on, it was time for gifts.*

later on 後來　　gift〔gɪft〕*n.* 禮物

　　　這句話的意思是「後來，拆禮物的時間到了。」
也可說成：

　　After a while, it was time to open the gifts.

　　（過了一會兒，拆禮物的時間到了。）

　　Later, I opened the gifts.

　　（後來，我打開禮物。）

　　Then everyone gave me their gifts.

　　（然後大家都把他們的禮物送給我。）

　　【*after a while* 過了一會兒　　then〔ðɛn〕*adv.* 然後】

3. *I couldn't wait to open it!*

wait〔wet〕*v.* 等

　　　這句話的意思是「我等不及要打開它！」也可說成：

　　I was eager to open it!（我渴望打開它！）

　　I was so excited to open it!

　　（我很興奮能打開它！）

　　I couldn't open it soon enough!

　　（我巴不得趕快打開它！）

　　eager〔'igɚ〕*adj.* 渴望的　　excited〔ɪk'saɪtɪd〕*adj.* 興奮的
　　soon〔sun〕*adv.* 快　　enough〔ə'nʌf〕*adv.* 足夠地
　　cannot…enough 無論怎樣…都不夠

4. *I couldn't help but laugh.*

help〔hɛlp〕*v.* 忍住
cannot help but* + *V. 忍不住…；不禁…
　(= *cannot help* + *V-ing* = *cannot but* + *V.*)
laugh〔læf〕*v.* 笑

　　這句話的意思是「我不禁大笑起來。」也可説成：

　　　　I couldn't stop myself from laughing.
　　　　（我忍不住大笑起來。）

　　　　I had to laugh.
　　　　（我不得不大笑起來。）

　　　　All I could do was laugh.
　　　　（我所能做的就只有笑。）

　　　stop〔stɑp〕*v.* 阻止
　　　stop* *sb.* *from* *V-ing 阻止某人…
　　　have to 不得不
　　　All one can do is V. 某人所能做的就是…

　　　help 的基本意思是「幫助」，在此是作「忍住」
解，與 can 或 cannot 連用。***cannot help but* + *V.***
的意思是「忍不住…；不禁…」，其用法舉例如下：

　　　　The bread smelled so good that
　　　　　I ***couldn't help but*** eat it.
　　　　　（這個麵包聞起來好香，我忍不住吃掉它。）

The story was so sad that I *couldn't help but* cry.
（這個故事太悲傷，我不禁哭了起來。）

The exam was so difficult that I *can't help but* worry about my grade.
（這個考試太難，我不禁擔心起我的成績。）

bread〔brɛd〕*n.* 麵包　　smell〔smɛl〕*v.* 聞起來
story〔'storɪ〕*n.* 故事　　sad〔sæd〕*adj.* 悲傷的
exam〔ɪg'zæm〕*n.* 考試
difficult〔'dɪfə,kʌlt〕*adj.* 困難的
worry about 擔心　　grade〔gred〕*n.* 成績

5. *It was the best present ever!*

present〔'prɛzn̩t〕*n.* 禮物　　ever〔'ɛvɚ〕*adv.* 至今

　　　這裡的 ever 是用來強調最高級，作「至今」解，所以這句話的意思是「牠是我有生以來最好的禮物！」也可說成：

It was the best present I had ever received!
（牠是我收過最好的禮物！）

It was the best thing they had ever given me!
（牠是他們給我的最好的東西！）

I had never received such a great present before!
（我之前從未收過這麼棒的禮物！）

receive〔rɪ'siv〕*v.* 收到　　never〔'nɛvɚ〕*adv.* 從未
great〔gret〕*adj.* 很棒的

另外，ever 的用法舉例如下：

① 用來強調最高級，作「至今」解。

That's the worst movie I've ***ever*** seen.

（那是我有生以來看過最爛的電影。）

② 用於疑問句，作「曾經」解。

Have you ***ever*** been abroad?

（你曾經去過國外嗎？）

③ 用於否定句，作「（不）曾；絕（不）」解。

I don't want to go back to that
restaurant ***ever*** again.

（我絕不想再回到那間餐廳。）

worst〔wɜst〕*adj.* 最糟的
movie〔'muvɪ〕*n.* 電影
abroad〔ə'brɔd〕*adv.* 到國外
go back to 回到
restaurant〔'rɛstərənt〕*n.* 餐廳
again〔ə'gɛn〕*adv.* 再

6. ***He is so much more than a birthday gift.***

more than 超過；不只是

這句話字面的意思是「他遠遠超過生日禮物。」
引申為「他絕不只是個生日禮物。」也可說成：

9

He is not just a birthday gift.

（他不只是個生日禮物。）

He is a birthday gift, and something more, too.

（他是個生日禮物，而且不只如此。）

He plays a much bigger role in my life than
that of a birthday gift.

（他在我的生活中所扮演的角色比生日禮物更加重要。）

something 〔'sʌmθɪŋ 〕 *pron.* 某物；某事

play 〔 ple 〕 *v.* 扮演　　big 〔 bɪg 〕 *adj.* 重要的

role 〔 rol 〕 *n.* 角色

7. *Gifts can brighten a person's day.*

brighten 〔'braɪtṇ 〕 *v.* 使變亮；使愉快

person 〔'pɜsṇ 〕 *n.* 人

這句話字面的意思是「禮物可以照亮一個人的一天。」引申為「禮物可以使人一整天都很愉快。」也可說成：

Gifts can make someone happy.

（禮物可以使人快樂。）

Gifts can cheer a person up.

（禮物可以使人振作。）

Gifts can make a person's day better.

（禮物可以使一個人的日子變得更好。）

【cheer 〔 tʃɪr 〕 *v.* 使振作 < *up* >】

 作文範例

An Unforgettable Gift

Getting gifts is a lot of fun, especially when they are a surprise. I have received many wonderful gifts in my life, but there is one that really stands out. It was given to me by my parents on my eleventh birthday, and it is the most unforgettable gift I have ever received.

On that day, my parents threw a party for me. After we all sang songs and ate the cake, they brought out their gift — a large white box with a red bow. I couldn't wait to open it! I quickly unwrapped it and, to my surprise, found a puppy inside! The dog kept barking at me and wagging its tail. I thanked my mom and dad for such a wonderful present.

I decided to name my dog Rover. I love to play with Rover, but I also take good care of him. I take him for walks in the park and help him to take a bath. I remember to feed him every day. Rover is a big part of my life. He is not just a birthday gift; he is my best friend. I will never forget my eleventh birthday, for it is the day Rover joined our family.

📖 中文翻譯

一份難忘的禮物

收到禮物是很有趣的，尤其是令人驚奇的禮物。我一生中收過許多很棒的禮物，但是有一個真的很突出。那是我十一歲生日時，我的父母送我的，而且它是我至今收過最令人難忘的禮物。

那天，我的父母為我舉辦一個派對。在我們唱完歌且吃了蛋糕之後，他們拿出他們的禮物——一個綁著紅色蝴蝶結的白色大盒子。我等不及要打開它！我很快地打開它，然後，令我驚訝的是，我發現裡面是一隻小狗！小狗不停地對著我叫，並搖著尾巴。我謝謝爸爸和媽媽送我這麼棒的禮物。

我決定幫我的狗取名為來福。我喜歡跟來福玩，但我也有好好照顧他。我帶他去公園裡散步，還幫他洗澡。我每天都有記得餵他。來福是我生活中很重要的一部分。他不只是一個生日禮物；他是我最好的朋友。我絕不會忘記我的十一歲生日，因為那是來福成為我們家庭成員的日子。

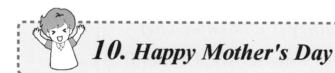

10. Happy Mother's Day

Attention, everyone.
I would like to say a few words.
Thank you very much.

It's Mother's Day today.
It's a day for celebration.
It's a day we honor our mothers.

I think my mom is amazing.
I would like to tell you about her now.
This is a toast to my mom.

Mother's Day	attention〔ə'tɛnʃən〕
would like	*a few*
word〔wɜd〕	celebration〔͵sɛlə'breʃən〕
honor〔'ɑnɚ〕	amazing〔ə'mezɪŋ〕
toast〔tost〕	

10

My mother is a talented chef.

It doesn't matter what I feel like eating.

My mother can cook just about anything.

She can make Chinese cuisine.

She can prepare Italian dishes.

Sometimes, she even cooks Japanese food!

Meals are never dull or boring.

Whatever we want, she can make it.

With her around, who needs restaurants?

---------------------------------- ------

talented ('tæləntɪd)	chef (ʃɛf)
matter ('mætɚ)	***feel like + V-ing***
just about	Chinese (tʃaɪ'niz)
cuisine (kwɪ'zin)	prepare (prɪ'pɛr)
Italian (ɪ'tæljən)	dish (dɪʃ)
Japanese (ˌdʒæpə'niz)	meal (mil)
dull (dʌl)	boring ('borɪŋ)
whatever (hwɑt'ɛvɚ)	around (ə'raʊnd)
restaurant ('rɛstərənt)	

My mother takes care of the housework.

There's a ton of things to do at the house.

Somehow, Mom manages to finish it all.

Our floors are always clean.

Our dishes are always spotless.

Our laundry is always neatly folded.

Sure we help out with a few things.

But Mom does the lion's share of the work.

Our house would be a disaster without her!

---

take care of	housework ('haʊsˌwɝk)
a ton of	somehow ('sʌmˌhaʊ)
manage ('mænɪdʒ)	finish ('fɪnɪʃ)
floor (flor)	spotless ('spɑtlɪs)
laundry ('lɔndrɪ)	neatly ('nitlɪ)
fold (fold)	sure (ʃʊr)
help out with	lion ('laɪən)
share (ʃɛr)	***the lion's share***
disaster (dɪz'æstɚ)	

10

My mother is also an accomplished driver.

During the day, I have many places to be.

Mom always gets me there on time.

She takes me to school in the morning.

She takes me to cram school in the evening.

She takes me to band practice

　　on weekends.

Mom is usually super busy.

But she finds time to drive me places.

I wonder how she handles everything!

---

accomplished (ə'kɑmplıʃt)

driver ('draɪvɚ)　　　　during ('djʊrɪŋ)

get (gɛt)　　　　　　*on time*

cram school　　　　　band (bænd)

practice ('præktɪs)　　weekend ('wik'ɛnd)

usually ('juʒʊəlɪ)　　　super ('supɚ)

wonder ('wʌndɚ)　　　handle ('hændḷ)

But most of all, *my mother is my best friend*.

I can tell Mom anything.

If I have troubles, she always hears me out.

She listens carefully to my problem.

She understands what I'm going through.

She tells me everything is going to

be okay.

I go to her when life has got me down.

She always lifts my spirits.

I always feel better after talking to her.

most of all	troubles ('trʌbḷz)
hear out	carefully ('kɛrfəlɪ)
problem ('prɑbləm)	
understand (ˌʌndɚ'stænd)	
go through	okay ('o'ke)
down (daʊn)	*get sb. down*
lift (lɪft)	spirit ('spɪrɪt)

10

In short, *my mother is a remarkable*
  person.

She always knows just what to say.

She's always there when I need her.

Thank you for being my mom.

I owe you my life.

I love you more than words can say.

My mother is a superwoman.

Let's toast her on her special day!

Happy Mother's Day, Mom!

---

in short	remarkable〔rɪˋmɑrkəbḷ〕
owe〔o〕	*more than*
superwoman〔ˋsupɚͺwʊmən〕	
special〔ˋspɛʃəl〕	

10. **Happy Mother's Day**

▪▪▪

🔊 演講解說

Attention, everyone.　　　　　大家請注意。

I would like to say a few words.　我想要說一些話。

Thank you very much.　　　　非常感謝你們。

It's Mother's Day today.　　　今天是母親節。

It's a day for celebration.　　這是值得慶祝的日子。

It's a day we honor our　　　這是我們要表揚自己的母親

　mothers.　　　　　　　　　的日子。

I think my mom is amazing.　　我覺得我媽媽很神奇。

I would like to tell you about　我現在想要告訴你們關於她

　her now.　　　　　　　　　的事。

This is a toast to my mom.　　這是要向我媽媽敬酒的祝詞。

** ─────────────────────

Mother's Day 母親節　　attention〔əˋtɛnʃən〕*interj.* 注意
would like 想要　*a few* 一些　　word〔wɝd〕*n.* 字；話
celebration〔͵sɛləˋbreʃən〕*n.* 慶祝
honor〔ˋɑnɚ〕*v.* 給…榮譽；向…致敬
amazing〔əˋmezɪŋ〕*adj.* 令人驚訝的
toast〔tost〕*n.* 敬酒時的祝詞

10

My mother is a talented chef.	我媽媽是一個天才廚師。
It doesn't matter what I feel like eating.	我想吃什麼都沒關係。
My mother can cook just about anything.	我媽媽幾乎什麼都會煮。
She can make Chinese cuisine.	她會做中國菜。
She can prepare Italian dishes.	她會做義大利菜。
Sometimes, she even cooks Japanese food!	有時，她甚至會做日本料理！
Meals are never dull or boring.	每餐絕不單調或令人厭倦。
Whatever we want, she can make it.	無論我們要什麼，她都會做。
With her around, who needs restaurants?	有她在身邊，誰還需要餐廳呢？

** ————————————————

talented〔'tæləntɪd〕*adj.* 有天份的　　chef〔ʃɛf〕*n.* 廚師
matter〔'mætə〕*v.* 有關係　　*feel like + V-ing* 想要…
just about 幾乎　　Chinese〔tʃaɪ'niz〕*adj.* 中國的
cuisine〔kwɪ'zin〕*n.* 菜餚　　prepare〔prɪ'pɛr〕*v.* 準備；烹調
Italian〔ɪ'tæljən〕*adj.* 義大利的　　dish〔dɪʃ〕*n.* 菜餚；盤子
Japanese〔͵dʒæpə'niz〕*adj.* 日本的　　meal〔mil〕*n.* 一餐
dull〔dʌl〕*adj.* 單調的　　boring〔'borɪŋ〕*adj.* 令人厭倦的
whatever〔hwɑt'ɛvə〕*pron.* 無論什麼
around〔ə'raʊnd〕*adv.* 在周圍；在附近
restaurant〔'rɛstərənt〕*n.* 餐廳

My mother takes care of the
　　housework.

There's a ton of things to do at
　　the house.

Somehow, Mom manages to
　　finish it all.

Our floors are always clean.

Our dishes are always spotless.

Our laundry is always neatly
　　folded.

Sure we help out with a few things.

But Mom does the lion's share of
　　the work.

Our house would be a disaster
　　without her!

我媽媽會做家事。

家裡有許多事要做。

不知道爲什麼，我媽媽總能
設法做完全部。

我們的地板總是很乾淨。

我們的盤子總是很潔淨。

我們洗好的衣物總是摺得很
整齊。

當然，我們也會幫忙做一些事。

但我媽媽會做大部分的工作。

如果沒有她，我們家就會亂
七八糟！

** ────────────────────

take care of 照顧；處理　　housework〔'haʊs,wɜk〕*n.* 家事
a ton of 許多　　somehow〔'sʌm,haʊ〕*adv.* 不知道爲什麼
manage〔'mænɪdʒ〕*v.* 設法　　finish〔'fɪnɪʃ〕*v.* 做完
floor〔flor〕*n.* 地板　　spotless〔'spɑtlɪs〕*adj.* 潔淨的
laundry〔'lɔndrɪ〕*n.* 洗好的衣物　　neatly〔'nitlɪ〕*adv.* 整齊地
fold〔fold〕*v.* 摺疊　　sure〔ʃʊr〕*adv.* 當然
help out with 幫忙完成　　lion〔'laɪən〕*n.* 獅子
share〔ʃɛr〕*n.* 一份　　*the lion's share* 最大的部分
disaster〔dɪz'æstɚ〕*n.* 災難；重大的失敗

10

***My mother is also an accomplished driver*.**　　　我媽媽開車的技術也很好。

During the day, I have many places to be.　　　在一天當中，我必須去很多地方。

Mom always gets me there on time.　　　媽媽總是能準時把我送到。

She takes me to school in the morning.　　　她早上要帶我去學校。

She takes me to cram school in the evening.　　　她晚上要帶我去補習班。

She takes me to band practice on weekends.　　　她週末要帶我去練習樂團。

Mom is usually super busy.　　　媽媽通常都非常忙碌。

But she finds time to drive me places.　　　但是她會找時間開車送我到很多地方。

I wonder how she handles everything!　　　我想知道她是如何處理每件事！

** ———————————

accomplished〔əˋkɑmplɪʃt〕*adj.* 技術高超的
driver〔ˋdraɪvɚ〕*n.* 駕駛人　　during〔ˋdjʊrɪŋ〕*prep.* 在…期間
get〔gɛt〕*v.* 把…送到　　**on time** 準時　　***cram school*** 補習班
band〔bænd〕*n.* 樂團　　practice〔ˋpræktɪs〕*n.* 練習
weekend〔ˋwikˋɛnd〕*n.* 週末　　usually〔ˋjuʒʊəlɪ〕*adv.* 通常
super〔ˋsupɚ〕*adv.* 非常　　wonder〔ˋwʌndɚ〕*v.* 想知道
handle〔ˋhændḷ〕*v.* 處理

But most of all, *my mother is my*　　但最重要的是，我媽媽是
　　best friend.　　　　　　　　　　我最好的朋友。
I can tell Mom anything.　　　　　　我可以跟媽媽說任何事情。
If I have troubles, she always hears　如果我有煩惱，她總是會
　　me out.　　　　　　　　　　　　聽我說完。

She listens carefully to my problem.　她會仔細聆聽我的問題。
She understands what I'm going　　　她了解我現在經歷的事情。
　　through.
She tells me everything is going　　　她告訴我一切都會沒問題。
　　to be okay.

I go to her when life has got me　　　當生活令我沮喪時，我會
　　down.　　　　　　　　　　　　去找她。
She always lifts my spirits.　　　　　她總是會振作我的精神。
I always feel better after talking　　　跟她談過之後，我總是會
　　to her.　　　　　　　　　　　　感覺好一些。

＊＊ ────────────────────────

most of all 最重要的是（= *most important of all*）
troubles〔'trʌblz〕*n. pl.* 煩惱　　***hear out*** 聽完
carefully〔'kɛrfəlɪ〕*adv.* 仔細地　　problem〔'prɑbləm〕*n.* 問題
understand〔͵ʌndɚ'stænd〕*v.* 了解　　***go through*** 經歷
okay〔o'ke〕*adj.* 沒問題的　　down〔daʊn〕*adj.* 沮喪的
get sb. down 使某人沮喪　　lift〔lɪft〕*v.* 振作
spirit〔'spɪrɪt〕*n.* 精神

10

In short, my mother is a
  remarkable person.
She always knows just what to say.
She's always there when I need
  her.

Thank you for being my mom.
I owe you my life.
I love you more than words can
  say.

My mother is a superwoman.
Let's toast her on her special
  day!
Happy Mother's Day, Mom!

總之，我媽媽是個了不
起的人。
她總是知道要說什麼。
當我需要她的時候，她
總是會在身邊。

謝謝妳成爲我的媽媽。
我的一生都要歸功於妳。
我愛妳超過言語所能
表達。

我的媽媽是位女超人。
讓我們在這特別的日子
裡舉杯祝賀她吧！
媽媽，母親節快樂！

** ——————————————

in short 簡言之；總之
remarkable〔rɪˋmɑrkəbḷ〕*adj.* 出色的；了不起的
owe〔o〕*v.* 欠；必須感謝；歸功於　　*more than* 超過
superwoman〔ˋsupɚͺwʊmən〕*n.* 女超人；能力非凡的女人
toast〔tost〕*v.* 爲…舉杯祝賀
special〔ˋspɛʃəl〕*adj.* 特別的

背景說明

　　每位母親幾乎都會打掃、洗衣服、煮飯等，好像沒有什麼家事難得倒她們。最重要的是，我們能出現在這個世界上，都要感謝母親辛苦地生下我們。每年的母親節，一定要記得謝謝自己的母親。

1. *This is a toast to my mom.*

   toast〔tost〕*n.* 敬酒時的祝詞

   　　toast 的基本意思是「吐司」，在此是作「敬酒時的祝詞」解。這句話的意思是「這是要向我媽媽敬酒的祝詞。」也可說成：

   　　This is a tribute to my mother.
   　　（這是對我母親的讚頌辭。）

   　　This is in honor of my mother.
   　　（這是要向我的母親致敬。）

   　　This is to celebrate my mother.
   　　（這是要讚頌我的母親。）

   　　tribute〔'trɪbjut〕*n.* 頌辭　　*in honor of* 向…表示敬意
   　　celebrate〔'sɛlə,bret〕*v.* 慶祝；讚頌

2. *My mother can cook just about anything.*

   just about 幾乎（= *almost*）

   　　這句話的意思是「我媽媽幾乎什麼都會煮。」也可說成：

10

My mother can make any dish.

（我媽媽什麼菜都會做。）

My mother can cook all kinds of food.

（我媽媽會煮各式各樣的食物。）

My mother is a great cook.

（我媽媽是一個很會煮菜的人。）

dish〔dɪʃ〕*n.* 菜餚　　kind〔kaɪnd〕*n.* 種類

all kinds of 各式各樣的　　great〔gret〕*adj.* 很棒的

cook〔kʊk〕*n.* 廚師

3. ***But Mom does the lion's share of the work.***

lion〔'laɪən〕*n.* 獅子　　share〔ʃɛr〕*n.* 一份

the lion's share 最大的部分

　　lion 的意思是「獅子」，share 的意思是「一份」，***the lion's share*** 字面的意思是「獅子的那一份」，引申為「最大的一份」，在此作「最大的部分」解。這句話的意思是「但我媽媽會做大部分的工作。」也可說成：

But my mother does most of the housework.

（但我媽媽做大部分的家事。）

But she does most of the chores.

（但她做大部分的家事。）

But she does most of the work around the house.

（但她做大部分的家事。）

housework〔'haʊs,wɝk〕*n.* 家事

chores〔tʃorz〕*n. pl.* 雜事　　around〔ə'raʊnd〕*prep.* 遍及

　　the lion's share 字面的意思是「獅子的那一份」，源自「伊索寓言」，獅子和其他動物獵到一隻獵物，獅子卻企圖把整隻獵物獨吞，因而引申為「最大的部分」。
其用法舉例如下：

Jimmy took *the lion's share* of the cake.
（吉米拿了最大塊的蛋糕。）

The lion's share of his wealth was inherited.
（他大部分的財產是繼承來的。）

Retirees make up *the lion's share* of the tourists on this trip.
（這次旅行的觀光客大部分是由退休的人組成的。）

wealth〔wɛlθ〕*n.* 財富；財產
inherit〔ɪnˈhɛrɪt〕*v.* 繼承
retiree〔rɪˌtaɪˈri〕*n.* 退休者　　*make up* 組成
tourist〔ˈtʊrɪst〕*n.* 觀光客　　trip〔trɪp〕*n.* 旅行

4. *Our house would be a disaster without her!*
disaster〔dɪzˈæstɚ〕*n.* 災難；重大的失敗

　　這句話字面的意思是「如果沒有她，我們家會是一個災難！」在此引申為「如果沒有她，我們家就會亂七八糟！」也可說成：

10

Our house would be a mess without her!

（如果沒有她，我們家會變得亂七八糟！）

But for her the state of our house would be
  terrible!（如果沒有她，我們家的情形會很糟！）

If it were not for Mom, we would live in
  a pigsty!

（如果不是媽媽在，我們就會住在髒亂的地方！）

mess〔 mɛs 〕*n.* 亂七八糟   ***but for*** 如果沒有

state〔 stet 〕*n.* 狀態   terrible〔'tɛrəbḷ 〕*adj.* 很糟的

if it were not for 如果沒有

pigsty〔'pɪɡˌstaɪ 〕*n.* 豬窩；骯髒的地方

5. ***My mother is also an accomplished driver.***

accomplished〔 ə'kɑmplɪʃt 〕*adj.* 技術高超的

driver〔'draɪvɚ 〕*n.* 駕駛人

　　accomplished 的基本意思是「完成的」，在此是作「技術高超的」解。這句話字面的意思是「我媽媽也是個技術高超的駕駛人。」引申為「我媽媽開車的技術也很好。」也可說成：

My mother is also a good driver.

（我媽媽也很會開車。）

My mother can also drive very well.

（我媽媽開車也開得很好。）

My mother is also a skilled driver.

（我媽媽的開車技術也很好。）

【 skilled〔 skɪld 〕*adj.* 熟練的 】

6. *If I have troubles, she always hears me out.*
   troubles〔ˈtrʌblz〕*n. pl.* 煩惱　　***hear out*** 聽完

   　　　trouble 的主要意思是「麻煩」，在此是可數名詞，作「煩惱」解。而 out 的基本意思是「向外」，在此是作「到最後」解，***hear out*** 的意思就是「聽完」。這句話的意思是「如果我有煩惱，她總是會聽我說完。」也可說成：

   　　When I have problems, she always listens.
   　　（當我有問題時，她總是會注意聽。）

   　　Whenever I am troubled, she listens to me.
   　　（每當我有煩惱的時候，她就會聽我說。）

   　　If I have troubles, she lets me talk.
   　　（如果我有煩惱，她會讓我說。）

   　　problem〔ˈprɑbləm〕*n.* 問題
   　　whenever〔hwɛnˈɛvɚ〕*conj.* 每當
   　　troubled〔ˈtrʌbld〕*adj.* 煩惱的

7. *She understands what I'm going through.*
   understand〔ˌʌndɚˈstænd〕*v.* 了解　　***go through*** 經歷

   　　這句話的意思是「她了解我現在經歷的事情。」也可說成：

   　　She understands what I am experiencing.
   　　（她了解我現在經歷的事情。）

   　　She knows what my life is like.
   　　（她知道我的生活狀況。）

   　　She understands my situation. （她了解我的情況。）

   　　experience〔ɪkˈspɪrɪəns〕*v.* 經歷　　　life〔laɪf〕*n.* 生活
   　　like〔laɪk〕*prep.* 像　　situation〔ˌsɪtʃuˈeʃən〕*n.* 情況

10

go through 作「經歷」解，其用法舉例如下：

I can only imagine what the earthquake survivors *went through*. （我只能想像地震的生還者經歷的事。）

Debbie is *going through* a tough time, so let's be nice to her.

（黛比正經歷艱苦的時刻，所以我們對她好一點吧。）

I didn't want to *go through* the ordeal of the exam, so I didn't register for it.

（我不想經歷考試的折磨，所以我沒有報名。）

imagine〔ɪˈmædʒɪn〕*v.* 想像
earthquake〔ˈɝθˌkwek〕*n.* 地震
survivor〔səˈvaɪvɚ〕*n.* 生還者　　tough〔tʌf〕*adj.* 困難的
ordeal〔ɔrˈdil〕*n.* 折磨　　exam〔ɪgˈzæm〕*n.* 考試
register〔ˈrɛdʒɪstɚ〕*v.* 報名 <*for*>

8. *I owe you my life.*
owe〔o〕*v.* 欠；必須感謝；歸功於

　　　owe 的基本意思是「欠」，在此是作「必須感謝」或「歸功於」解。這句話的意思是「我應該為我的生活感謝妳。」或「我的一生都要歸功於妳。」也可說成：

I owe you everything. （我所有的一切都要歸功於妳。）

I wouldn't be here without you.

（如果沒有妳，我就不會在這裡。）

Everything I have is because of you.

（我擁有的一切都是因為妳。）

 作文範例

Happy Mother's Day

Today is Mother's Day, the day we honor our mothers. Like most people, I think my mom is amazing, and I would like to express my appreciation to her.

I appreciate my mother for all of the things she does. *For example*, she is a talented chef and can cook anything I want. Meals at our house are never dull. *In addition*, she takes care of the housework. Although we all try to help out, it is Mom that does the lion's share of the work. Without her, our house would be a disaster. She also drives me wherever I need to go no matter how busy she is. It makes me wonder how she handles everything. Best of all, my mother is my best friend. I can tell her anything, and she always lifts my spirits.

In short, my mother is a remarkable person. I owe her my life and love her more than words can say. It is not nearly enough, but all I can do is say Happy Mother's Day!

10

📖 中文翻譯

母親節快樂

　　今天是母親節，是我們該向自己的母親致敬的日子。像大多數的人一樣，我認為我的母親是很神奇的，所以我想對她表示感激。

　　我感謝我的母親所做的一切。例如，她是個天才廚師，而且她會煮任何我想要的食物。我們家的每一餐絕不會單調。此外，她也會做家事。雖然我們大家都想要幫忙，但媽媽總是做最多的工作。如果沒有她，我們家就會一團亂。無論她有多忙，她也會開車送我到任何我必須去的地方。這讓我很想知道，她是如何處理每件事。最棒的是，我母親是我最好的朋友。我可以跟她說任何事，而她總是能振作我的精神。

　　總之，我母親是個了不起的人。我的一生都要歸功於她，而且我愛她超過言語所能表達。這根本不夠，但我能做的，就是說一聲母親節快樂！

這10篇演講稿，
你都背下來了嗎？
現在請利用下面的提示，
不斷地複習。

以下你可以看到每篇演講稿的格式，
三句為一組，九句為一段，每篇演講稿共
六段，54句，看起來是不是輕鬆好背呢？
不要猶豫，趕快開始背了！每篇演講稿只
要能背到一分半鐘之內，就終生不忘！

1. My Winter Vacation

Hi, ladies and gentlemen.
I love winter vacation.
It's nice to have lots of ....

There's so much ....
There's so much ....
There's so much ....

What do I do?
What activities ....
Let me tell you!

I can relax all day.
I can turn off the ....
I can sleep late.

There's no need to ....
No need to jump ....
I can sleep as late ....

I can sit on the sofa ....
There's no pressure.
I can relax and enjoy!

I can go traveling.
I don't have to ....
There are so many ....

I can travel ....
I can even travel ....
The sky is the ....

I can just pack ....
I better remember ....
I'm sure I'll ....

I can meet my friends.
It's a chance to ....
I can meet them ....

I can meet my friends ....
I can meet my friends ....
I can meet my friends ....

The city is a ....
We're sure to ....
We'll never ....

I can play sports.
I can go ....
I can get ....

Maybe I'll ....
Maybe I'll ....
I just hope ....

Sports are ....
They can keep ....
They are also ....

I can spend time with ....
My family is very ....
I need to be ....

I can visit ....
I can visit ....
I'll bet they will ....

Winter vacation is special.
It's a wonderful ....
I like it the best!

2. My Interests

Hello, ladies and gentlemen.
We are all special.
We all have our own interests.

Maybe we like ....
Maybe we like ....
There are just ....

Today, I would like to ....
I'd like you to ....
I'd like to tell you ....

I really like music.
I love listening to songs.
I love watching music videos.

Music is wonderful.
It can ....
It can ....

I can ....
I can ....
Music puts me ....

I really like movies.
I like ....
I like ....

Sometimes I like ....
Sometimes I like ....
Sometimes I like ....

Movies are ....
The stories are ....
The actors are ....

I love to read.
I love reading ....
Reading takes me ....

There are ....
There are ....
There are ....

I can also ....
Good books can ....
Who says learning ....

I like playing games.
They can be ....
They can be ....

I always try ....
There's no need ....
Games are only fun if ....

It doesn't matter if ....
I always have ....
Games can bring me ....

I have many interests.
My interests make ....
I enjoy them very much.

I know I can't ....
Working hard is ....
But sometimes I ....

We can find our own interests.
We can learn more about them.
They can make life ....

3. My Favorite Country

Welcome, ladies and gentlemen.
It's nice to see all of you.
I hope you are all feeling great.

My speech today is ….
It's a place that is ….
It's a place that is ….

I would like to tell you ….
It is located just ….
My favorite country ….

Canada is a very clean country.
It has a lot of ….
It has a lot of ….

There are many ….
There are a lot of ….
Canada is known ….

Canadians try to ….
They like to ….
Canadians care ….

Canada is also very ….
Many different kinds of ….
Everyone lives ….

It doesn't matter …..
It doesn't matter ….
They live together ….

Going to Canada is special.
We don't just get to ….
We can see almost ….

Canadians are also very polite.
They are ….
They are ….

Canadians often say ….
Canadians like to ….
Canadians don't like to ….

Good manners make life ….
Canada is famous for this.
It's a very nice place to be.

Finally, Canada is a ton of fun!
There's always something ….
We'll never get bored.

We can go ….
We can go ….
We can go ….

The leaves even ….
It's very pretty!
Canada is a beautiful place.

I think Canada is a ….
Its scenery ….
Its people ….

I love Taiwan.
It will always ….
But I think Canada ….

Traveling can be a lot of fun.
Canada is a perfect place ….
I hope I can go to Canada soon!

4. My Favorite Song

You all have arrived ....
We will begin soon.
Thank you for coming.

My favorite song ....
It is a major part ....
Sometimes I hear it ....

This song brings ....
I can express ....
Here are some ....

The song is about me.
I heard it once ....
The words ....

After hearing it, I ....
It lifted me up when ....
I listened to it before .....

Now I listen to it ....
It helps me ....
I love to sing ....

It is also a song to exercise to.
Frankly, its ....
It helps me push ....

At the end I have ....
My power is ....
I feel fantastic!

Some people do not like it.
They say it gives them ....
But I think it helps me.

Also, *its tune is* ....
I can sing it ....
My voice is ....

My friends sometimes ....
But I keep ....
It is impolite, but ....

Sometimes, my friends ....
I tell them ....
They do not always ....

Finally, *my song* ....
I remember when ....
Those were ....

I realize how lucky .....
I hear the music and ....
It is easier to ....

Some bad memories ....
But my song makes ....
It pushes the ....

It is good to have ....
You will become ....
Listen closely and ....

It must have ....
The rhythm is ....
Most important ....

My favorite song helps me.
I think everyone should ....
They always mean a lot!

5. My Favorite TV Show

Hi, ladies and gentlemen.
It's nice to see everyone here.
Thank you very much ....

Almost everyone watches ....
There are so many ....
But in my mind, one ....

It's a show that ....
It's truly one of ....
Let me tell you about ....

Wild Kingdom teaches us ....
There are so many ....
The show can teach us ....

We can learn how ....
We can learn how ....
We can learn how ....

Each animal is unique.
Each one has its ....
Wild Kingdom lets us ....

We can also learn ....
Wild Kingdom is ....
But there are subtitles ....

We can improve ....
We can increase ....
We can even improve ....

Wild Kingdom can ....
If we want to, we can also ....
Just listening to the show ....

Wild Kingdom is ....
It's watched by ....
Even babies can ....

The show is very ....
It is okay for ....
It is easy to ....

Wild Kingdom is for people ....
It doesn't matter if ....
I mean, who doesn't ....

But most of all, the show is ....
Wild Kingdom is ....
Watching animals is ....

Wild animals can ....
Wild animals can ....
Sometimes, wild animals can ....

Wild Kingdom is very ....
There's no telling ....
The show keeps us ....

In short, Wild Kingdom is ....
It is my favorite ....
There's something ....

We can watch almost ....
But Wild Kingdom is ....
Wild Kingdom is very ....

Would you like to find ....
Do you like shows that ....
Be sure to watch Wild Kingdom!

6. The Internet and I

Please make yourselves ....
It's nice that we could ....
Please sit back and enjoy ....

The best mass media is ....
It can provide so ....
People use it to ....

The Internet has ....
I would like to ....
Here goes!

First, the Internet gives ....
I can visit ....
There is information ....

I can learn ....
I can watch ....
I can find ....

I can learn ....
I can watch ....
With the Internet ....

Also, I can stay in touch.
E-mail and ....
It is just like ....

I am able to ....
I can hear about ....
News from around ....

Blogs bring ideas ....
I can log on and ....
My blog gives me ....

Third, many games are ....
Some I can ....
Some I can .....

The best games are ....
They are exciting.
They let me enter ....

Many games are ....
They keep up ....
Spending time ....

Finally, it can help me ....
I can read stories ....
There is no need to ....

There are also many ....
Downloading music ....
Full albums cost ....

I can read ....
There is no cost ....
They are all cheaper ....

The Internet is an excellent tool.
But it requires ....
Its many functions ....

I use it for everything ....
It's better than ....
Anyone can see ....

The Internet is a ....
We can do so much with it.
I can no longer imagine ....

7. *Stress in Teenagers*

Good evening, ...
Thank you for being here.
It's nice to see you.

Teenagers today are ....
There are many things ....
It's not easy ....

My speech today is ....
It's something that ....
Stress in teenagers is ....

First, what is stress?
It is worry or strain ....
We can get stress ....

We can feel stressed ....
We can feel stressed ....
We can even feel stressed ....

Teens have a lot of ....
Teens have many exams ....
Teens today are ....

So, what can stress ....
The effects of stress ....
Every teenager handles ....

Some teens ....
Some teens ....
Others can even ....

Stress is powerful.
Stress can affect ....
It makes teenagers ....

Stress can also affect our bodies.
Many effects can be ....
Here are some ....

Our palms may start ....
We could feel butterflies ....
Our hearts may start ....

Some teens may start ....
Others may even break ....
Teens have to be aware .....

So, what can teenagers do ....
There are many things ....
Here are some ....

We can train ....
We can try ....
We can talk ....

Most of all, we can try ....
Sometimes bad things ....
We just have to ....

Stress is everywhere.
It is a part of our ....
We can't escape it.

But stress isn't always ....
Without stress, we ....
Without stress, nothing ....

Teenagers shouldn't try to ....
We should just try to ....
Take a deep breath and relax!

8. *A Letter to the Principal*

Hello, ladies and gentlemen.
Thanks for taking the time ....
I hope that you will enjoy ....

I really like ....
Sure it gets ....
But school can be ....

The other day, I decided to ....
This letter was to ....
Here's what it said.

Dear Principal Lee,
How are you?
Are you busy?

I'm sorry to ....
I know you have ....
But there's something ....

I'm writing you this ....
I think people don't ....
But there are many ....

Thank you for my teachers.
My teachers take care ....
They teach me about ....

They teach me ....
They teach me ....
They even teach me ....

My teachers are ....
They seem to know ....
I hope I will be as ....

Also, thank you for ....
I've made so many ....
We have a great ....

We have lunch together.
We study together.
We sometimes even ....

I cherish each of ....
I'll never forget ....
They will be in my ....

Finally, thank you for ....
Learning is so important.
School is where learning ....

I learn how to ....
I learn about ....
I get wiser ....

School prepares me ....
There are many ....
I think my school ....

In closing, it's great to ....
It has taught me ....
It has made me ....

I'll keep ....
I'll keep ....
I won't let myself ....

School is such a special time.
Junior high only comes once.
I will try to make the most of it!

9. An Unforgettable Gift

Getting gifts is a lot of fun.
It's always a big surprise!
There was one gift that ....

Today, I'd like to ....
I hope you enjoy ....
It is a story about ....

My parents threw me ....
All of my friends were ....

We sang songs.
We ate birthday cake.
It was a wonderful time.

Later on, it was time ....
My parents had promised ....
I was so excited!

It was wrapped ....
There was a big red ....

Mom placed it ....
She told me to be ....
I couldn't wait ....

There were holes on ....
I wondered what ....
I quickly unwrapped ....

I was so surprised!
It was so cute!

The dog kept ....
Its tail wagged ....
It jumped up and ....

I couldn't help ....
I thanked my ....
It was the best ....

Rover is a very ....
He loves to ....

I take him for ....
Rover likes to be ....
I think they like ....

I help him take ....
I feed Rover ....
Rover is a big ....

He is so much more than ....
He is my best friend.

He was the best present ....
I'll never forget my ....
It was the day Rover ....

10. Happy Mother's Day

Attention, everyone.
I would like to say a few words.
Thank you very much.

It's Mother's Day today.
It's a day for ....
It's a day we honor ....

I think my mom is ....
I would like to tell you ....
This is a toast to my mom.

My mother is a talented chef.
It doesn't matter what ....
My mother can cook ....

She can make ....
She can prepare ....
Sometimes, she even ....

Meals are never ....
Whatever we want, she ....
With her around, who ....

My mother takes care of ....
There's a ton of things ....
Somehow, Mom manages to ....

Our floors are always ....
Our dishes are always ....
Our laundry is always ....

Sure we help out ....
But Mom does the lion's ....
Our house would be a ....

My mother is also an ....
During the day, I have many ....
Mom always gets me ....

She takes me to ....
She takes me to ....
She takes me to ....

Mom is usually ....
But she finds time to ....
I wonder how she ....

But most of all, my mother ....
I can tell Mom ....
If I have troubles, she ....

She listens carefully to ....
She understands what ....
She tells me everything is ....

I go to her when life ....
She always lifts ....
I always feel better after ....

In short, my mother is a ....
She always knows ....
She's always there ....

Thank you for ....
I owe you my ....
I love you more ....

My mother is a superwoman.
Let's toast her on her ....
Happy Mother's Day, Mom!

臺中市 102 年度國民中學學生英語演講比賽實施計畫

主辦單位	一、指導單位：教育部 二、主辦單位：臺中市政府教育局 三、承辦單位：臺中市立光復國民中小學
演講題目	1.The Best Movie I Love 2.The Ways To Keep Healthy And Happy 3.My Plans In My School Life

高雄國際聯青社辦理 102 年「高雄地區中等學校第 43 屆英語演講比賽」

主辦單位	一、主辦單位：高雄市高雄國際聯青社 二、指導單位：高雄市政府教育局
演講題目	題目與時間： A. 高中組 　題目：Living at a moment 　演講時間：五分鐘、英文即席問答：30-40 秒 B. 國中組： 　題目：Super power 　演講時間：三分鐘、英文即席問答：30-40 秒

台中市立光榮國民中學 101 學年度光榮國中英語演講比賽題目

演講題目	1. A Wonderful Summer Vacation. 2. The Teacher That I like Most.

彰化縣英文研究推廣協會 2012 菁英盃

指導單位	彰化市公所
主辦單位	彰化縣英文研究推廣協會
演講題目	國中二年級組：Helping People Is Happy 國中一年級組：Live Happily 國小高年級組：Computer And I 國小中年級組：A Cell Phone 國小低年級組：My Best Friend

臺北市 101 學年度高中學生英文作文暨高國中學生英語 演講比賽實施計畫

主辦單位	一、主辦單位：臺北市政府教育局（以下簡稱本局） 二、承辦單位：臺北市立育成高級中學

演講題目	(一) 高中組
	   1. 演講題目
	    (1) 指定題：How I Will Introduce Taipei to Foreigners?
	      （參賽學生不得使用輔助圖片或道具）
	    (2) 看圖即席演講：由本局聘請命題委員命題，於比賽當場宣布，準備時間 5 分鐘。
	   2. 演講時間
	    (1) 指定題：4 分鐘。
	    (2) 看圖即席演講：2 分鐘。
	(二) 國中組
	   1. 演講題目
	    (1) 指定題：My Plan for High School Life.
	      （參賽學生不得使用輔助圖片或道具）
	    (2) 看圖即席演講：由本局聘請命題委員命題，於比賽當場宣布，準備時間 20 分鐘。
	   2. 演講時間
	    (1) 指定題：3 分鐘。
	    (2) 看圖即席演講：2 分鐘。

彰化縣 101 學年度國民中學英語演講暨朗讀比賽實施計畫

主辦單位	一、主辦單位：彰化縣政府教育處。 二、承辦單位：彰化縣立信義國民中小學。 三、協辦單位：彰化縣九年一貫課程教學英語輔導團。
演講題目	① The Best Book I Have Ever Read ② What Can We Do To Protect Our Earth

高雄市岡山國中 101 年度英語演講比賽題目範圍

主辦單位	高雄市岡山國民中學
演講題目	題目範圍： Some people prefer to spend their free time outdoors, and others prefer to spend their free time indoors. Which one do you prefer? Use specific reasons and examples to support your answer. 依題目範圍，比賽當天抽選題目進行即席演講。

2012 年高雄市中等學校第四十二屆英語演講比賽辦法

主辦單位	一、主辦單位：高雄市高雄國際聯青社 二、協辦單位：高雄市基督教青年會（YMCA） 三、指導單位：高雄市政府教育局
演講題目	高中組： 題目：An Embarrassing Moment 演講時間：五分鐘、英文即席問答：30-40 秒 國中組： 題目：My School Uniform 演講時間：三分鐘、英文即席問答：30-40 秒

2012 年青商盃大二林地區英文演講比賽

主辦單位	主辦單位：二林國際青年商會
演講題目	國小組、國中組 MY family　我的家人 My favorite school subject　我喜歡的學校科目 The man I will never forget　我最難忘的人

101 年宜蘭縣國立臺灣大學校友會—第 15 屆英語演講比賽

演講題目	1. 國小組：How can I make my parents happy? 2. 國中組、高中組、高職五專：What can I do to help my classmates learn better English? 3 國外組〈A 組〉：採不事先公佈，當場抽題。準備時間 5 分鐘，會場提供字典。

天主教道明高級中學 101 學年度國中英文演講校內比賽

主辦單位	教務處教學組
演講題目	初賽題目：Keeping a Pet 順序：由教務處教學組以電腦亂數隨機排列另行公佈。 決賽題目：採即席演講，當場抽題方式。

2011 第四屆環球盃英語演講比賽

主辦單位	主辦單位：應用外語系暨應用外語系學會
演講題目	請選擇其中一題自行撰寫演講內容。 高中職組： How I use Facebook to connect to the world. How my school protects our environment. How Taiwan promotes our indigenous culture. How my school is working to stop bullying. Why nuclear power is a good way to make power. Why nuclear power isn't a good way to make power. 國中組： Students in my school spend too much time on Facebook. How I protect our environment. How my school is working to stop bullying. What I would change about my school. What I would change about my hometown.

「一口氣英語基金會」贊助各校英語演講比賽得獎同學名單

名次	姓名	學校班級	獎學金
1	林佳宏	建國中學 118	5000
1	鍾靈	建國中學 222	5000
1	何秉宸	建國中學 124	5000
1	余典翰	建國中學 225	5000
1	李瑜庭	建國中學 223	5000
1	李穆先	北一女中二儉	5000
1	孫彤	景美女中一美	5000
1	江妍	景美女中二樂	5000
1	郭文馨	景美女中二樂	5000
1	喻曄庭	中正高中 221	5000
1	謝欣晏	大同高中 211	5000
1	邱世耀	成淵高中 111	5000
1	張博爲	成淵高中 207	5000
1	鍾靈	建國中學 108	5000
1	何秉宸	建國中學 219	5000
1	黃嘉宇	建國中學 119	5000
1	曾子巍	建國中學 206	5000
1	徐嘉陽	中崙高中 10824	5000
1	張祐寧	中崙高中 20330	5000
1	林念純	中正高中 121	5000
1	吳威辰	弘道國中 81029	5000
1	李玉觀	弘道國中 813	5000
1	袁麗儀	永吉國中 814	5000
1	張天胤	中正國中 818	5000
1	蕭世揚	台中三光國中 209	5000
1	邱奕銓	台中忠孝國小 513	3000
1	廖士喆	台中惠文國小 506	5000
2	紀少庭	建國中學 115	3000
2	張興舜	建國中學 224	3000
2	盧偉博	建國中學 128	3000
2	張晉瑋	建國中學 207	3000
2	江衡	建國中學 220	3000
2	林姝含	北一女中二良	3000
2	陳彥均	景美女中一誠	3000
2	許珈華	景美女中二樂	3000
2	王怡云	景美女中二樂	3000
2	蕭宇珊	中正高中 221	3000
2	丁彤	大同高中 214	3000
2	朱純瑩	成淵高中 111	3000
2	黃川容	成淵高中 111	3000
2	張興舜	建國中學 120	3000
2	黃柏源	建國中學 218	3000
2	李果恆	建國中學 111	3000
2	李冠瑩	中崙高中 10803	3000
2	樊千	中崙高中 20914	3000
2	徐之顏	中正高中 221	3000
2	戴偉哲	弘道國中 81345	3000
2	呂瑞琪	弘道國中 810	3000
2	廖卿閔	永吉國中 815	3000
2	鄧涵云	中正國中 812	3000
2	蔡欣曄	台中三光國中 201	3000
2	廖珮辰	台中忠孝國小 506	2000
2	蔡婷瑋	台中惠文國小 614	3000
3	彭俊人	建國中學 122	1000
3	鄭凱文	建國中學 209	1000
3	黃柏源	建國中學 123	1000
3	陳韋豪	建國中學 206	1000
3	呂新禾	北一女中二忠	1000
3	何宛庭	景美女中一樂	1000
3	王薾萱	景美女中二善	1000
3	李茉	景美女中二義	1000
3	洪薇安	中正高中 121	1000
3	吳佳燕	大同高中 212	1000
3	黃彥凱	成淵高中 102	1000
3	莊凱琪	成淵高中 107	1000
3	陳思翰	建國中學 116	1000
3	林嘉興	建國中學 221	1000
3	李晏廷	建國中學 116	1000
3	葛忠祥	中崙高中 10231	1000
3	陳欣茹	中崙高中 20118	1000
3	黃鈺雅	中正高中 121	1000
3	曾亭瑄	弘道國中 81617	1000
3	雷雅云	弘道國中 805	1000
3	游士衡	永吉國中 810	1000
3	鄭瑋心	中正國中 801	1000
3	吳姿瑩	台中三光國中 207	1000
3	許再臨	台中忠孝國小 414	1500
3	陳冠宇	台中惠文國小 608	1000
4	郝立中	建國中學 127	500
4	陳昱翰	建國中學 202	500
4	劉耘非	建國中學 101	500
4	陳宜宏	建國中學 217	500
4	羅簌	北一女中二眞	500
4	林怡德	景美女中一樂	500
4	徐之顏	中正高中 121	500
4	黃笠淇	大同高中 209	500
4	江傳助	成淵高中 104	500
4	方敏	成淵高中 205	500
4	李宇璿	建國中學 127	500
4	周靖安	建國中學 224	500
4	張思維	中崙高中 10808	500
4	邢蘭杰	中崙高中 203	500
4	郝逸豐	中正高中 216	500
4	林冠妤	弘道國中 80704	500
4	陳彥伶	弘道國中 809	500
4	游承彥	永吉國中 803	500
4	趙育誠	中正國中 810	500
4	吳姒穎	台中三光國中 208	500
4	蕭皓云	台中惠文國小 508	500
4	仲崇遠	台中三光國中 212	500
4	楊恩朋	台中忠孝國小 514	1000
5	王子毅	建國中學 128	500
5	巫天允	建國中學 211	500
5	楊凱文	建國中學 113	500
5	蔡博安	建國中學 225	500
5	吳書衡	建國中學 203	500
5	吳星玫	北一女中二義	500
5	周奇葳	北一女中二平	500
5	胡育鳳	北一女中二樂	500
5	李品萱	景美女中一和	500
5	孔令揚	景美女中二和	500
5	郭蔚霖	中正高中 201	500
5	黃奕勳	大同高中 213	500
5	許皓陽	成淵高中 111	500
5	陳安迪	成淵高中 212	500
5	巫明翰	建國中學 113	500
5	陳柏宇	建國中學 209	500
5	張芩浩	建國中學 229	500
5	美娜	中崙高中 104	500
5	安思雅	中崙高中 204	500
5	黃凡修	中正高中 121	500
5	賀瓔萱	弘道國中 80410	500
5	連培安	弘道國中 813	500
5	張詠哲	永吉國中 812	500
5	楊睿安	中正國中 823	500
5	蕭深深	台中忠孝國小 601	800
5	洪偉倫	台中惠文國小 601	500
6	李奕聰	台中忠孝國小 403	500
優勝	吳秉儒	台中忠孝國小 406	200
優勝	林郁霏	台中忠孝國小 408	200
優勝	周昀頡	台中忠孝國小 611	200
優勝	曾鼎睿	台中忠孝國小 505	200
優勝	曾心慈	台中忠孝國小 503	200
優勝	姚晴文	台中忠孝國小 515	200

國中生英語演講 ②

主　　　編 / 劉　毅

發　行　所 / 學習出版有限公司　　☎ (02) 2704-5525

郵　撥　帳　號 / 0512727-2 學習出版社帳戶

登　記　證 / 局版台業 *2179* 號

印　刷　所 / 裕強彩色印刷有限公司

台　北　門　市 / 台北市許昌街 10 號 2 F　　☎ (02) 2331-4060

台灣總經銷 / 紅螞蟻圖書有限公司　　☎ (02) 2795-3656

美國總經銷 / Evergreen Book Store　　☎ (818) 2813622

本公司網址　www.learnbook.com.tw

電　子　郵　件　learnbook@learnbook.com.tw

售價：新台幣二百八十元正（書＋CD）

2013 年 5 月 1 日一版二刷

ISBN 978-957-519-969-2　　　　版權所有 · 翻印必究